C'EST LA GUERRE

C'EST LA GUERRE

LOUIS CALAFERTE

TRANSLATED FROM THE FRENCH BY
AUSTRYN WAINHOUSE

THE MARLBORO PRESS/NORTHWESTERN
NORTHWESTERN UNIVERSITY PRESS
EVANSTON, ILLINOIS

The Marlboro Press/Northwestern
Northwestern University Press
Evanston, Illinois 60208-4210

Originally published in French in 1993 under the title *C'est la guerre*. Copyright © 1993 by Éditions Gallimard. English translation copyright © 1999 by Austryn Wainhouse. Published 1999. All rights reserved.

Printed in the United States of America

ISBN 0-8101-6032-3 (cloth)
ISBN 0-8101-6068-4 (paper)

Library of Congress Cataloging-in-Publication Data

Calaferte, Louis, 1928–
   [C'est la guerre. English]
C'est la guerre / Louis Calaferte : translated from the French by Austryn Wainhouse.
   p. cm.
ISBN 0-8101-6032-3 (cloth). — ISBN 0-8101-6068-4 (paper)
   1. World War, 1939–1945—France—Fiction.   2. France—History—German occupation, 1940–1945—Fiction.   I. Wainhouse, Austryn. II. Title.
   PQ2663.A389C4713   1999
   843'.914—dc21   99-13415
                                                       CIP

C'EST LA GUERRE

La gue-rre
La gue-rre
La gue-rre
C'est pas pour s'amuser

Y a des soldats qui tombent
Y a des soldats qui meurent
On les met dans les tombes
Ils sont morts avant l'heure

On ne veut plus de guerre
Jetez-leur donc des bombes
On les mettra en tombe
Ceux qui font la misère

La gue-rre
La gue-rre
La gue-rre
C'est pas pour s'amuser

—French anarchist song from the
nineteenth century

FIVE O'CLOCK IN THE AFTERNOON ON A LUKEWARM
and overcast September day.

The tocsin sounds.

Our playing comes to a stop.

Black dress buttoned up to her neck, arms raised,
bony white hands, eyes staring, the old woman screeches
on the village square that they've called a general mobilization.

Not a breath of air stirs in the leaves of the big tree.
Some birds are chirping.

Standing at attention in his overalls, hands in his
pockets, a man is crying.

He has on wooden shoes.

There is noise and there is silence, but the silence
swallows up the sounds. It's the way it is at burials.

A long black cat is stretched full length on a win-
dowsill.

Two elderly women are hugging each other, each
with her head in the hollow of the other's neck. The bun

belonging to the shorter one has come undone, her gray hair falls in long wavy strands on either side of her shoulders. Live eels, that's what they look like. I need to pee.

From somewhere far off comes a heifer's plaintive lowing.

Some villagers stand leaning back against a building's soiled yellow facade.

Sitting on a stone, the little girl in blue is holding her ball on her lap with both hands. Her white socks are sunk down in bunches around her ankles. She is biting her lips.

In front of the little drystone wall a woman has knelt down on the sand of the square. Her hands are joined, her back is bent over, her head bowed. It's like a church statue, but black.

My pants are too short for me, they bind between my legs, on my knees I've got some big scabs, there's still a little pus or blood that keeps oozing out and it stings.

The grocer and his wife are standing on their doorstep in their gray smocks.

A red kite winks up in the sky.

Some men arrive. They shake hands. You see them talking to each other, nodding their heads, shaking their heads, shrugging.

Two women have set their metal pails full of water on the ground and are standing there behind them, arms hanging at their sides.

I haven't had my afternoon snack. I am hungry.

The little redheaded boy is scooting around on all fours in the dust, blowing spit bubbles. He receives a kick, falls forward on his stomach, and bursts out laughing. The kick was from his mother. She pulls him to his feet, yanking him up by his arm. She flicks at the dust on his black school smock, slaps him. He cries.

—Smacking kids, you don't do that on a day like today, says an old man, it being war.

I don't know what general mobilization means, but I am very pleased about it being war.

I am eleven years old.

—The bastards, one man is saying.

What I like is the bread sliced thick with salted butter and a sugar cube on it.

A tall woman comes up.

—But I knew it! I just knew it!

Her hair, which she wears cut short, seems to be sizzling all around her head.

—I wrote somebody a letter this morning. Instead of putting the right date on it, I put 1914 for the year—twice!

I gaze at her, lean, anxious, wide eyed, with that loud voice. I don't understand what she's talking about, but to me she looks pretty dumb.

—Papa served in 1914!

—So did my father, says a young peasant with blond hair on his bare chest.

—And now we're good for it once again, says the man with the mustache.

I have to go home to get my snack.

—I'm wondering whether they've even received the notices at the town hall.

—What notices?

—The general mobilization notices. They're required to put them up.

—Put them up where?

—On the door of the town hall and on the door of the gendarmerie. They've got to post them.

—What's the point of that, since we already know?

—That's just how it is. It's required.

The old woman with the bent-over back breaks into tears.

—Oh, my little ones! My little ones!

The biggest of the men puts an arm around her shoulders and draws her close. He is looking off into the distance.

—All right Grandma all right Grandma.

His huge hand shuts on the old woman's shoulder.

—Oh, 'tis a great pity. A great pity.

The tall woman is somewhere in the middle of all the people. You hear her screeching voice.

—I've got to see my children right away. I've got two sons, you hear? Two boys old enough to fight. I want to see them before they go off.

A friend comes up to me. What are we going to do with our marbles, he asks, if this is war?

In the street with the rounded paving stones I pee against the milestone. My pee splashes on it and then trickles away yellow.

Everyone has stopped work.

The grown-ups are talking.

They are waving their hands in the air.

You'd say they were afraid of something.

On the houses the roofs are a reddish color.

Smoke is coming out of a chimney.

High-pitched women's voices scratch at the heaviness over everything.

A yoked team of red oxen waits by the pool.

A man is cleaning out the inside of his wooden shoe.

A rubber ball comes rolling by.

Drops of my pee are wetting my legs.

There are the kids.

—So what are we playing?

—How about war.

A man nearby has overheard us. I receive a kick in my rear end.

I'd like for him to die in the war.

—Not going to be any snack today. I haven't had the time to fix it. And it's not enough for you to have to blubber about it. If this is war, you're going to be seeing worse than that.

Ordinarily calm, the skinny little woman seems to have become electrified.

—And don't just stand in the way, get out from under my feet! In the hall I almost bump into the big man of the house, who pats me gently on the head.

—This is war.

He takes off his black cloth cap with the leather

visor. Clumps of hair stick together from the sweat on his pale scalp.

At the end of the hall I watch myself making faces in the mirror hung on the wall, and in a low snarl I utter the words:

—This is war! . . . This is war! . . . This is war! . . .

I spring into the air, give the mirror a lick of my tongue, I don't feel good, it seems to me something is hurting inside one of my ears, I go quietly up to the attic to snitch an old apple off the layer of blackened straw, I take a bite, the apple tastes like vomit, I spit it out, I wipe at my tongue with the palm of my hand, I fling the apple as hard as I can off into the darkness at the back of the attic, it squishes against some wall or a big wooden chest, there are big wooden chests stacked up back there, I look down at my shoes, it seems to me I smell of urine, I shuffle my shoes two or three times in the straw which turns into dust, I feel queasy, I think of what they say about ghosts that wander in the attic at night, I feel frightened, I start running, I am alone, I don't feel good.

—My father was wounded in '16.

—I lost my two brothers, in '16 and in '17.

—In '14 there were nine of us in the house. By the time they signed the Armistice only two were left. And of course I didn't get back in what you'd call great shape.

—The idea was there wasn't going to be any more war.

—That was supposed to be the very last we'd have.

—It's political, that's the thing.

—Well, I'd say Daladier did what he could.

—He did try to arrange things, that's for sure.

—Politicians can't do everything they'd like, in politics it's the same as it is everywhere else.

—The Boches, say what you like it's always going to be the Boches.

—But what I'm saying is that if it continues this way there's never going to be an end.

—You've got to think of our dead.

—As a widow I can tell you what they're good for, those Boches.

—Bunch of dirty bastards.

—By God, if I'd been Daladier, I'd have shown them a thing or two! By God I would!

—Daladier's somebody, all right.

—I'm not saying he isn't. But even so.

—It isn't for nothing they called him the Bull from Vaucluse.

—Whatever, it's still politics, the whole thing, and what's politics isn't clean.

—And it's always the same ones who have to pay.

—What you've got to understand is that we're all in the shit now.

—Well, we're just going to have to make Hitler eat it.

—And the really rich stuff, while we're at it.

—Hitler, he's out of his mind.

—Reminds you of Charlie Chaplin.

—Me, I just want to tell you, I don't believe in any Hitler.

—Maybe you don't, but the results are there.

—The Boches, maybe they are all a bunch of bastards, but we've got our fingers on the trigger too.

—What do you mean, we? You're exempted.

—And the curé isn't?

—The curé, for him and us it's the same, curés go to war.

—At the front you got to have curés.

—I'm against that, personally.

—You're against it, you're against it, but when you're hit in the belly and you've got your guts spilling out all over the place, maybe you're pretty damned glad if they have a curé nearby.

—Myself, it's the pope I don't go for.

—Mustn't talk against the pope, it's bad luck.

—What's clear to me in all that is that my son's going to have to go, he's of age.

—That's what's clear to me too.

—My sister-in-law's two boys have been called up already.

—If it was left up to me, fighting a war is something that people would do a lot less of.

—You don't have any say in the matter.

—We're in for a squabble no matter what.

—Nowadays it's airplanes and tanks.

—Cold steel against cold steel, that's what they said it would be.

—Don't worry, everything they say is pure crap. You think we're going to bleed each other to death like we did in '14?

—And just what the hell are you going to do, wise guy, when your papers come telling you to report?

—Maybe I'll report the same as the others, but this filthy war of theirs, it's something I don't give one little goddamn about.

—We aren't the only ones in this mess, the English are in it too.

—The English, sure, they're our allies, but we haven't the foggiest idea what they have in mind.

—There's Chamberlain.

—Right. He's not worried, he's got his umbrella.

—Good God, you can say what you like, it's still a rotten thing to have happened.

Someone has carried a table and some chairs out into the street in front of the house. A woman has set two bottles of red wine and some glasses out there. Some men have sat down. Some men are standing. Some women are behind the men. The white dog is curled up on the pavement, asleep. One child is playing with a yo-yo. One child has a hoop. One child has a scooter. One child has on a little yellow straw hat. One child's mouth is smeared with chocolate. They are talking. They are pounding on the table. They are snorting. They are scratching under their arms. They are scratching their heads. They are tilted back in their chairs. They stick their thumbs under their suspenders. They pretend but they are not all right, not comfortable. They scrape their fingernails upon the wooden tabletop. They talk. They understand each other. And yet, just what does that mean, '14, what does the Armistice mean, what does Daladier mean, the Boches are what, Hitler is what, politics is what, what is the Bull of Vaucluse, what is Chamberlain, what is the pope, what is war?

—What is war?
—Just mind what's on your plate. Eat.

What war is, well, to start with it's when you're in the middle of having a good time on the big square squatting down with the others around the Tour de France circuit traced on the ground that you have to go all the way through by tossing your agate each time it's your turn more than one can be playing it it's even better if several are and then the more you are the more agates you can win a big agate's worth two little ones you need ten marbles to get one agate or else seven new marbles but I don't like to trade I prefer my agates some of them I even stole I didn't win them all I stole them from the ones from the notary's who sometimes come out in the street to play they aren't allowed to their parents have said they can't they say it's dirty it's low class but even so they've got agates little ones and big ones especially a really good big one that I didn't steal I won it out of the pot they aren't used to playing with ones like us and so they aren't very good winning their marbles is easy it's too bad their mother doesn't let them come out more often they told us their parents bought them all the agates they wanted they also have a little red car which climbs up walls if you want they showed it to us on Sunday because on Sunday they go to mass at ten o'clock with their maid who is big and who laughs all the time when there are boys around her during that time they come with us a little before going inside the church the rest of us go to the eight o'clock mass they told us that the ten o'clock mass is for rich people the war, well, maybe it's there won't be any more masses either at eight o'clock or at ten o'clock but I don't believe it mass is dear God the Father and little Jesus they don't have anything to do with the war or maybe when they ring the tocsin the war, well, it's when we're all on the big square, everybody and when there are some who are crying not to mention the grown men but war, well, it's when you realize that something is in the middle of happening which doesn't happen every day when it must be serious as the big man of the house says war with his cap shoved back we're in for more sufferings again, yes, when it's war does the war take place even when you go to sleep, well, it's really been quite a day not like usual perhaps tomorrow will be the same sort of day there is even somebody who said there mightn't be school anymore just like that when it's war.

We are in the dining room. I'm supposed to help by handing up to the big man of the house the gummed paper strips he is crisscrossing over the panes in the window, the way we have already done in the two bedrooms and have to do in the kitchen, wherever there are windowpanes which can bust during the bombing raids.

—What you got to get into your head is that this time it won't be the same tune as in '14, says the big man of the house while he carefully applies the strips of paper, feet perched on the sill.

—Now don't go and fall, says the skinny little woman.

—I'll be the first one wounded in the war, ha ha! says the big man of the house. You, hey, hand me the paper instead of watching the flies fly around.

Do the flies know that this is war?

Do flies fight wars?

How would a fly go about fighting a war?

A fly could bombard, it's flying, it flies over some houses and *bloum!* It drops its bombs.

—Today's bombs, there's nothing they won't tear apart, says the big man of the house.

You can tell that the skinny little woman is really frightened. For a long moment she keeps still, then she says that we're in a world where people have gone crazy.

—Come on, you wouldn't have had us lie down and just take a screwing from the Boches, would you, the big man of the house says as he leans dangerously out the window.

—Watch what you're doing, says the skinny little woman. You fall, and it won't be the Boches who'll be picking you up out of the bean patch.

After nightfall, with the wooden shutters closed, lights inside make all those bandages on the window-panes stand out.

While you're eating you can't prevent yourself from looking at them, but you don't understand what use they'd be if there was a bombardment.

A bombardment, that would be houses collapsing, and if houses collapse, even with sticky paper windows will collapse too.

They ought to explain how this bombardment would be.

Whatever, there mustn't be any light that could be seen from Boche airplanes coming over at night.

Tomorrow the big man of the house plans to paint all the windowpanes blue, because tomorrow is Sunday, but the skinny little woman doesn't agree.

—And how will I be able to see in order to sew? Eh? Because, war or no war, things will always have to be sewn, for sure.

—It's a civic duty, says the big man of the house.

He isn't accustomed to those words.

He repeats.

—It's a civic duty.

Nobody knows what that is supposed to mean.

There's silence now, but we understand that it's something important.

In the soup plate the soup is green.

There's a wind. It bites your legs.

—We'll be served everything at once, the war along with the cold, you hear an old man say underneath his black hat.

Coming out of the house this morning I thought there was a smell of flowers in the air. There are almost no flowers left at this season of the year. The guys are sitting on the benches in the public garden.

—My father's leaving tonight.

—Mine is too.

—Seems there'll be trucks for them to go off in.

—Mine's leaving by train. My mother's got his kit all packed.

—Mine too. She filled it full of scarves and socks for the winter.

(Where are the soldiers when it snows?)

—My father said in the other war his father had been in the hell of the trenches and you had to put on plenty of clothes if you didn't want to freeze from head to foot.

—My father said that in the army they provide everything. And anyway, he said, the war isn't going to last long.

—Mine said that since the Boches are all a pain in the ass he'll kill as many of them as he can.

(What kind of feeling must it give you to kill people?)

—My father's already got stripes in the army. He's a field corporal.

—Mine said the army is made up of nothing but loafers.

—If I was grown up I'd go and kill the Boches.

(I wouldn't like to have anybody to kill.)

—Why do they call them the Boches?

—Because that's the name they have.

(Suddenly I catch on that the Boches are the Germans.)

—My mother says that all alone in the house with the five of us it's going to be hard.

(I wonder whether in war they pay the soldiers.)

—Us, we've got the farm. To take care of all that

maybe we'll have to stop going to school.

—Tomorrow night my mother and my brother we're all going to go with my father to the station.

(How do they know when the fathers are dead in the war?)

—Maybe when we're grown up we'll have to go there too.

(The war, where is it at?)

—My father says if everybody got together there wouldn't be any more war.

(Who says there has to be war?)

—They say the Boches cut off the children's hands.

(How do you cut off a hand?)

It's warm in the kitchen. We had soup with bits of bacon in it, and cheese and grapes. The skinny little woman cleared off the table. The big man of the house invited the neighbors over to listen to the radio. They don't have one at their place. On the sideboard there's a set. Streamlined. In wood, with two knobs underneath a dial which gives off a little green light when you turn the radio on and which has all the cities of the world written on it next to numbers. It's with the radio you hear Daladier's speeches. There's one this evening. The neighbors are coming over. The skinny little woman will get out the bottle. It'll be warm and cozy. It'll start humming in your head. They'll tell us to go to bed meanwhile the big man of the house will be saying that there's never been the likes of the Bull of Vaucluse that with him Boches or no Boches there isn't anything to worry about.

The forest is deep. In it the light is dim. You hear faint rustlings all around. Dried twigs and layers of dead leaves crackle or sink underfoot. You are alone amid these woody odors. It could make you afraid. I am not afraid. If I am ever a soldier in the war I mustn't be afraid. I have gone into the forest on purpose to find out whether I'd be afraid. Yesterday the skinny little woman said it's awful all these young men who are going off one after the other. She felt sorry for them but you could also tell that she admired them. I would like to go off so I'd be admired. I receive no attention. The mushrooms with orange hats are not edible. They are *poisonous*. Snakes are *venomous*. In certain countries the snakes are as big as the trunks of trees. I have seen pictures of them. All they have here is vipers. I know how you take hold of them. By grabbing them tight behind the head between your thumb and your first finger. The big man of the house has taught me about vipers. About how to whittle whistles out of elder branches. About how to catch fish in the stream with your bare hands. The big man of the house also taught me about kites. Vipers don't frighten me. The silence of the forest doesn't frighten me. I am not afraid of anything. I am a soldier. The war does not make me afraid.

Deserted streets of the village early in the morning. In front of the blacksmith's it smells of scorched horse's hoof. In front of the bakery it smells of warm bread. The big public fountain trickles. Going past, you stick your hand in. The water is ice cold. On the stone lip around it the moss is yellow-green and black. If you have any chalk in your pocket you write your name on the lip. You're not allowed to but everybody does it. Someone has written capitalist war in big letters. It's a pain not to understand everything. The tailor has not opened his shop. On the door is a piece of cardboard held by a string. The tailor is *mobilized*. I wouldn't mind having a piece of cardboard on our door but the big man of the house is too old to go to the war I heard him say. You go to the war at what age? Maybe if I said I wanted to be in the war they'd take me? The skinny little woman would *ready my kit* for me and I'd *join my unit*. Whom do you ask? Cats, they're always skinny. They get stones thrown at them. They meow and they climb up wherever like a flash. The yellow cat sitting on the step in front of the store is called Bobtail, its tail was cut off. A sharp wind's blowing. It's the north wind. Clattering on the pavement, a sharp sound, a sound of slipperiness too. It's the horse that belongs to Monsieur the Collector of Revenues. A man always in the streets on his red-and-white horse with long slender legs a cloth jacket with a straight collar black boots. He sits stiff on his saddle and waves hello only to men never to women or to children people take off their cap or their hat to say hello to him from down below when he goes by on his big horse from his look he doesn't seem to see anybody. I don't like him. He lives in a big house on a dead-end street. You could get in there and break his windows but we don't dare. The big man of the house says that Monsieur the Collector of Revenues spoke to him yesterday afternoon. The skinny little woman says my goodness me it flusters her to think that Monsieur the Collector of Revenues would have addressed himself to the big man of the house. He drew up his horse and he said that the war was going to mean hardships for everybody that there were dark days to prepare for. What are *dark days?* Out in the direction of the cemetery you see the whole valley the green of the meadows making the cows stand out that are grazing or that are lying down in twos or threes. If I had fifty centimes I'd go buy some eucalyptus cigarettes at the sisters' home. The first puff makes you cough but afterward it's a nice sugary kind of odor in your mouth and in your nose. If I help him the big man of the house gives me ten centimes sometimes twenty-five. At the end of the street there's the post office. Do you write letters when you're at the war? At the post office they have put a flag out. A blue white red. The wind is making it flap. It would be good if I had a flag. If I had one all the guys would want to trade me for it. The skinny little woman says all the time that I am a liar. I like to invent stuff. For instance with the words they say that you don't know you invent stuff the way it is in war the pack a soldier carries the Lebel the forced marches the trenches the sergeant the puttees the bayonet the hand-to-hand the shell holes the mess the infantrymen the baggage master the captain the chaplain the permissions the HQ the nighttime reconnaissances the surprise attacks the sentries the dugouts the hand lantern sometimes at night in bed I'm the sergeant or the grunt I have a bayonet in the trenches I attack.

The notices are white with big black letters and smaller ones.

At the top is a little pair of crossed flags.

They stand still there in front of them hands behind their backs arms dangling.

They have hard faces.

It's like the women don't dare come up too close.

It's inside a wooden frame behind a wire mesh.

From far off you can only read the big letters.

There are a lot of them and even so they make no sound.

The jaw clenches on the one who is white faced and who has thick black hair brushed back.

The air is chilly but they are in shirtsleeves.

It goes on for some time.

They separate in silence.

The women don't dare look at them.

Each one heads off alone toward where he lives.

It's the way it is when one returns from visiting somebody who has died.

The butcher at the pork shop has hung himself.

Night has fallen.

Everybody's running to his shop.

I have a sore tooth.

The door is open.

Long tables.

Hooks and knives.

Yellow light.

A lot of people are already there.

You hear a woman crying.

There is also a crying child.

The woman who's crying is sitting on a chair surrounded by other women who are holding her hands.

The woman who's crying keeps saying he told me he

told me if they go to war I'll hang myself if they go to war I'll hang myself he told me so.

A little gray dog is licking her feet.

At the back of the emptiness in there hangs the dark shape of a man.

He has on slippers.

—The pork butcher's hung himself, says the skinny little woman.

—Did you see him?

—I didn't want to see him. Someone hanging, it isn't a pretty sight.

—My husband saw him. He hung himself from a hook. Alongside the pig.

—His chin had gone all blue.

—The war's to blame, said the skinny little woman.

—He told me. He said if there's a war I'm hanging myself.

—And by God he did it, said the big man of the house.

—There you are, that's what war is, said the skinny little woman.

—He was to join his unit.

—This war you don't know what it's going to turn into.

—They were wanting too much, the Boches. First Austria, then Danzig. And after that why not us?

—Some people are saying it isn't going to last. When Hitler sees he's got the whole world against him he'll sober up.

—Yeah, well, he still has to be taught a lesson.

—And you wouldn't want the butcher to have hung himself for nothing.

There is a big gray house that I really like.

Once you're in bed before you fall asleep you think about what you saw during the day about what you did about what you heard about the look on people's faces about the man who has this one eye that's looking up in the air and whom the guys are scared of and me too I'm scared of him but his eye up in the air it sort of grabs hold of me he was talking with the garage mechanic he was saying that with the bad luck of having an eye like that there was some good luck too that with his eye stuck up in the air that way they didn't want him in the army and that just worked out fine because him and the war it was like oil and water it was one hundred percent shit this war was did we even know why it was being fought for the arms manufacturers and the arms manufacturers the more it's fought the fatter they get them and their women who suck their money out of them and that's not all they suck while we're marched off like cattle to the slaughter and shit that's what it all finally comes down to taking us for assholes that stuff's not going to work forever we haven't got fuck-all to do with this arms-manufacturing bastards' war Cachin said it in so many words but instead of listening to him they listen to those right-wing sons of bitches who've got the employers in their pocket they couldn't find anything better to do than fight another war for them the people we're nothing but so much cheap meat let them go fight it themselves their filthy

21

fucking war I'm not ashamed to say it luckily I've got my eye otherwise I'd desert the first chance I got and there's others I know who'll do like me but you won't hear a word about them it's like the ones they shot in '17 they let on there was only one or two of them the truth is they had to shoot them by the thousands just about everywhere it's all shit through and through the rich on one side and the others on the other side it's always been that way since the world began but you're not going to see me falling for this crap of theirs it'll be our turn someday those are Cachin's own words this eye of mine is a burr up their ass when I'm in bed I stick it right up there before I go to sleep you think again about the whole business it's kind of frightening ever since the war started things are kind of frightening.

The bedroom has blue wallpaper with birds flying in the sky.

There will be air raids with civilians as targets, airpower will be what counts, nevertheless the infantry will have to be reckoned with, as always, you wage war first of all with men, the side with well-trained troops that's who's sure to carry off the ribbon, the foot soldier is what you have to put your money on, machines, even perfected ones, can't do everything, and to run machines you need men, it's men first and foremost and it will always be that way in no matter what sort of a war, disciplined troops and good officers leading them, as regards leaders we've got what it takes, it's not that sure, nobody has already proven himself the way the great ones did in '14, if those guys were still around we wouldn't have anything to worry about, but the bombing of cities, that's the most dangerous, Hitler has said he'd level everything, he's capable of doing it, the man's a bandit, there'll be gas of one sort or another, we had that at the end of the last one, if they drop that on cities with the women and children they're real bastards, they'll pay for it, there's such a thing as justice for God's sake, it's not for nothing we have a League of Nations, Hitler though he is he too will end up by obeying, he'll have to, who're you kidding, Hitler doesn't give a good goddamn about the League of Nations, he's hot shit, he's got his army and he'll go the whole way, with him it's discipline discipline, that's why the Boches have got it all together, it's not the way it is here where it's a fucking mess wherever you look, with our damned Yids behind every crooked operation, I'd say there's a bit of tidying to be done there, naturally we're not on the side of the Boches but if they can help clean out the stables it won't hurt, there are too many of them who have profited from this, who've used it to fill their pockets and who continue to stretch things, and now they're ready to break, there'll be some ugliness, it wouldn't be bad to have a clean country once again, you've seen the names they've got, nothing but foreign names you aren't even able to pronounce.

They are drinking wine.

A nicely dressed little girl has arrived from Paris.

—Your father, eh? Where is he?

—My father says you can go stick it.

—He's not in the army, your father? He doesn't fight when there's a war?

—My father has already fought in a war.

—Liar.

—Screw you.

—To begin with, nobody's ever set eyes on your father.

—Screw you.

—Maybe you haven't got a father, huh?

The two Boutelleau boys left this morning, Adrien, the tall one, Marceau's son, young Laigneau, the Martin boy, the one in the Brérot family, that Alexandre boy, that Henri one, the Batailleur boy, André's son, Fréchot, Montard, one of the Rogers, Porchereau, Berger's going tomorrow, this morning I saw his mother, the poor woman, they might as well have cut off one of her arms, us women don't see any rhyme or reason to the things you men get yourselves into, but one thing I do understand, it's that war oughtn't to be allowed.

The skinny little woman's all choked up, she takes off her glasses, she wipes her eyes with her handkerchief, her nose is red.

On the road which leads to the station there's a tiny little house with just one window.

By threes or fours the men go past, kit bag on their back.

Some with a pair of brogans hanging from one shoulder by their knotted-together laces.

They are silent.

At the front door of the tiny house, a rosary between her fingers, the old lady is murmuring God preserve you my little ones God preserve you my little ones.

The trickles of tears look as if they had dug down into the creases in her cheeks on each side of her nose.

The men pass by, none daring to look at her.

They walk the way you do when you are compelled to.

You get the feeling they feel ashamed.

At the church guild's meeting on Thursday the priest has us take seats in the auditorium. Big voice, authoritarian. We must be patriots. A patriot's somebody who loves his native land. Our native land is the country we were born in, where our parents and all our ancestors were born, worked, suffered, died, and were buried. Men's native land is their mother. The way Jesus had a mother, the Virgin Mary, we too have a mother, but our native land is the mother of us all. Our native land is France. France is the most beautiful land in the world. It is the land of Joan of Arc, of Saint Vincent de Paul and of Father de Foucauld. God loves France. God defends France. God protects France. God will save her. We must love God and France our native land. We are to suffer for her and, if we have to, die for her. To die for one's native land is a special God-given grace. Maybe among our dads who have left for the front and who are going to take their weapons in hand and fight, maybe there are some who will get themselves killed by the serpent which is the enemy. We must pray for our daddies to all come back safe and sound and covered with glory, but should it ever turn out that one of them falls on the field of honor, that will be out of love of our native land, therefore out of love for God, and he will go straight to Heaven, accompanied by the band of angels which will scatter rose petals about him forever. We who because we are children have not gone off to fight in the war nevertheless have duties, duties toward our families as we do toward our native land, our beautiful native land of France, which has nourished us with the riches of its past. We are its sons, we are to love it as we love God and serve it as we serve God. All the saints are watching us, we must not disappoint them by behaving badly, they must be proud of us every day. The French blood in our veins does not belong to us, it belongs to France. To be French is to be a child of God. We must defend our land against those who seek to pillage and enslave it. Starting today, a roll will be called on Thursdays and each of us will give news, if he has had any, of his daddy who is at the front. Should a misfortune befall a family fellowship shall bind us to it and we shall support it in its sorrow. If one of our comrades has a name from another country, and if he says bad things about France, the following Thursday we must report the fact to His Reverence. And now let us pray together for our soldiers.

They roll their cigarettes between their fingers, they have fingers that are thick and act a little stiff. Crumbled sprigs of tobacco lie near the edge of the table. The cigarette once made, they collect the leftovers carefully, using the edge of the hand, and sweep them back into the pig's bladder pouch that they then fold up and stick into their pocket, the cigarette stuck behind one ear. They take hold of it delicately between two fingers so as not to crush it. They seize it between their rounded lips and light it amid big puffs of bluish smoke. The ribbed glass is always halfway full of wine. They take a swallow and then running the back of their index finger along their lips or mustache give them a quick little wipe. They can remain for quite some time without saying a word. The café is brown from smoke. There's a sour smell. Outside, evening is coming on. A dog receives a kick. It whines. An old man comes in. He shakes hands around the table, drags a chair over, and sits down with the others. A woman with ruffled-up hair who walks scraping her feet on the floor brings him a glass. Her breasts are ready to bust out of the neck of her dress. Big white breasts, with a red stain on one that looks like an injury that was not well taken care of. She moves off, her ass sways from one side to the other. All of them follow her with their eyes.

—Ought to give her to Hitler, that'd hold him for a while.

They laugh.

—You guys talk, but there's not one young fellow left in the whole area.

They pour themselves wine.

—I never would have thought we'd see another one.

—God almighty, neither did I.

—To have gone through what we went through, all that just so as to have it happen again.

One of the men lifts his cap and with the other hand scratches his head.

—Right back into the same goddamned mess.

The discussion stops. They drink.

—That there Léon Blum, according to him there wasn't going to be a war, isn't that right?

—Your Blum and your Daladier, they're all one and the same.

—If I had to do it over again I'd vote for the other one, the uh . . . what's his name?

—Same damned difference.

—Uh, that other, what the hell's his name?

He hunts for the name, furrows upon his brow. He is unable to come up with it. The proprietress puts a new liter of wine down on the table.

—Tits like those, I wouldn't mind going for a little nap in there.

—The place is already taken.

—One of the ones on the left . . . I've got his name on the tip of my tongue.

—I'd prefer to have something else on the tip of my tongue.

Shoulders shake from partly stifled laughter.

—The leadership, if they'd had any balls, they shouldn't have let Hitler get away with it.

—There's certainly more to it than just Hitler, there's certainly other ones behind him.

—There's the Wops.

—Mussolini. Ah. There's a clown for you.

Glasses are refilled.

—The Wops, they're not the most dangerous.

—No, usually too busy shitting in their pants.

They drink.

—Saw that in Ethiopia. Yet they weren't up against anything but niggers.

—And in Greece.

—Greasy Guineas.

The bell tower strikes the hour.

—Time to head home for supper. The missus is expecting me. If I'm not on time, whoa! Look out.

They drain their glasses.

—It's Mama who won't stop crying. If she doesn't pull herself together, she's going to get sick on us. We haven't heard one word from them, we don't even know where they are.

—Hey, here's my little nipper coming to get me. That means the missus is getting impatient.

Outside in the street, in front of the door to the café, they all shake hands.

—With this war on nobody's interested in our old games of cards.

The houses are straight and stiff.

The Crucifixion at the top of the hill.

The stone Christ is suffering. His mouth twists from pain.

The grass is flattened down.

Brownish.

The wind flings itself in stinging gusts at your cheeks and bare legs.

The setting sun is a big blood-balloon inside the purple and black of the woolly clouds.

The earth is hard.

The little pebbles press into your knees.

I came to ask the little Jesus for it not to be war anymore.

—These peasant children, the lot of them should leave with their fathers, it would be good riddance.

The green lady has a dress which covers her ankles, a cane with a goose's head, and a stick which she holds her glasses up to her eyes with to look at you.

—To begin with, they are dirty.

I plant myself in front of her.

—I'm not dirty! I'm not a peasant child!

She moves me aside with the tip of her cane. Her servant follows her. In church she passes the holy water to her.

—That one's insolent to boot.

In her hand she holds a big purse of dark red velvet.

—Wars do after all have their good side.

Before her the servant opens the iron gate to the house which has such beautiful flowers in summertime.

—Little snotnose.

The gate closes. You can never see anything besides a little garden with, where it ends, four steps in front of the house.

Sometimes, in the evening, you hear music as you go by.

She's a wicked lady.

Perhaps the war will make her die.

The skinny little woman says that the people from Paris will be here tomorrow. That the downstairs has to be got ready for them and an extra bed fixed up in the attic for the children. They have seven children. Seven little girls.

—They want to put them out of harm's way, says the big man of the house.

The skinny little woman shrugs.

—The mother is afraid there'll be air raids.

—Come on, they're not going to bomb Paris, says the big man of the house. That'd really take the cake!

The skinny little woman loads pinecones into the cookstove.

—In Paris they know more about things than we do.

The big man of the house sits down at his place at the end of the table. He lays his cap on a chair.

—They don't have the right to bomb Paris.

I admire the big man of the house who knows all these things. The skinny little woman doesn't know as much as he does. Women know less about things than men. Later on I too shall be a man. I'll know like the big man of the house does whether Hitler has or hasn't the right to bomb Paris. I sit down next to the big man of the house. He and I, we're men, the two of us.

—If they ask me to look after the little girls I don't know what I should tell them.

The big man of the house is cutting the bread. The knife has a big shiny blade.

—Can't turn them away.

—In the cities they've got it worse than we do, says the skinny little woman.

—It's the cities they target first.

—That's what I was telling you.

The big man of the house has piled some slices of bread next to his plate.

—Yes, but not Paris. Paris is a capital. It's the capital of the world.

The skinny little woman pokes up the fire. She has beaten the eggs in the big bowl for the omelette. She puts the frying pan on the stove to heat and drops in a lump of butter which sputters.

I am hungry.

She is shrieking from grief in the courtyard of the farm.

She is holding her head with both hands.

It looks like she's about to fall.

She doubles over.

She straightens up.

Tears are gushing from her eyes.

Her whole face is wet.

She has crazy eyes.

She is shrieking.

She's missing a tooth at the front of her mouth.

With the flat of her hand she is hitting herself hard in the stomach.

They gather around her.

She pushes them all away.

She is slobbering.

She is stamping her feet.

She shuts her eyes.

She is in pain.

She falls to her knees.

Her son died at the railway station in Mulhouse.

He got underneath a train.

The police constable who has come to announce the news doesn't know what to do with himself now.

He has his kepi in his hand.

The husband is trying to lift her up.

She is beating the ground with her fists.

She throws herself down flat on the ground.

She wants to die.

She is screaming.

We dug this big hole. There's room for four of us in there. We placed branches and leaves on top. You're really sheltered inside. We took some bread, some cheese, and some chocolate. I have a brand-new knife with eight blades that was given to me by the big man of the house. The big man of the house made me a rifle out of wood. It has a trigger. At the bottom of the hole we put down straw and a blanket. And down there we've put some stones too. The stones, they're grenades. The grandfather of one of the guys showed him. You pull out the *pin* with your teeth, you count to ten, and you throw the grenade. After throwing it you lie down flat so as not to be hurt by the explosion. You keep inside the hole except for your head. We throw the grenades. The big man of the house paid us a visit. He told us we should be good soldiers and we should kill lots of Boches. I killed fifty. With grenades and with my rifle. *We retired to our positions.* That's how they say it on the radio. In the evening the first thing is the *communiqué.* In the evening and in the morning. They say all the time: *Nothing to report.* Next they say that our troops have *retired to previously prepared positions.* Airpower is the only thing we don't have. We don't know about building planes. *Our aircraft intervened effectively above the German lines.* You'd need to build an airplane out of the big containers for oil that the garage mechanic has. I asked the big man of the house. He said he didn't have the time. He told me that the rifle, that was enough for killing Boches. We don't have tanks either. *Our armor breached the enemy lines.* They say *armor. Tanks,* that's better. You see it better. We can make a tank by pushing a piece of sheet metal ahead of us, if a couple of us get together, but the piece belongs to the garage mechanic's son, and his father doesn't want to give it to us. Even without tanks and without planes, we'll win. The Boches won't come out on top. His Reverence told us they won't. God's children, they are the children of France. We must pray to God for victory.

The big man of the house doesn't mind if I look at the newspaper. Children needn't know what's written in the newspaper. Crimes or nasty stories. Now, though, children can see the pictures of soldiers arriving by train *somewhere in France.* They have a helmet hanging from their belt, their rifle hung over a shoulder by a strap. They have a big knapsack and big shoes. One who is very tall and very strong is holding a liter of wine in his outstretched hand. Behind him, another is drinking out of a bottle. In a corner of the picture there's a gendarme. The others are standing or squatting, their caps are askew on their heads. They look amazed to be there, not yet used to the uniform. They look kind of dumb, and also as if they were sleepy. There, you see, the boys are starting to check in, some of them, says the big man of the house. France isn't yet beaten by those pile-of-shit Prussians. Prussians, I know about them. The big man of the house has talked about them with the neighbors. In the picture, a soldier in the front row is holding a rabbit in his arms. That's the *mascot,* says the big man of the house. The skinny little woman asks why that soldier who's in front has brought a rabbit along to the war. Because it's the mascot, that's why. In war you always have a *mascot.* It's to bring good luck. In '14, the big man of the house had a little dog. A little dog that was black with a white spot under its neck. It wasn't a dog that was his alone, the dog belonged to the *section.* It had given them lots of laughs. Its name was Roodoodoo. One could say that, by way of a job, he'd landed a pretty soft one for himself. Each tried to give him more treats than the others. The big man of the house set up a sort of hut for himself at the end of the trench. He used to take Roodoodoo along when he went there for the night. He had found some straw and made a bed for him. On the day of the big attack Roodoodoo disappeared. Nobody knows what became of him. They retreated. They had other things to do than worry about him. There's a Negro soldier in the picture in the paper. With a funny-looking cap standing up on his head. It's called a *chéchia*. It's red. The Negroes, they have them wear that on their head, because they are Negroes. You don't need that to recognize them, says the skinny little woman, since they're Negroes. In the army, can't have everybody doing whatever they want, that'd be disorder. The Negroes, they put a *chéchia* on them. The big man of the house knows how they do things in the army. You're glad there's somebody who's able to explain.

—She didn't get over it. From the time her son went off she wasn't the same. They found her in the well.

—Their goddamned war, says an old man.

Strange names: Molsheim, Guebwiller, Forbach, Sarreguemines, Erstein, Altkirch. In the Bas-Rhin, the Haut-Rhin, the Moselle, is where they are. That's Lorraine, Alsace. The Boches are not going to take them back from us.

The viper writhes on the ground. It is gray and blue. We stab its head and body with a branch whittled to a point. It thrashes around. It tries to get away. It flings its head to the right, to the left. It leaps into the air. It falls back to the ground with a soft sound. It spits something white. It squirms. It gets stabbed in the neck. Its eyes are little black buttons. It slaps its tail against the ground. From so much rolling around in the dust it turns whitish. Its tiny tongue hangs out of the corner of its mouth. It's dragging in the dust too. Its struggles go on a long time. We stab it. That tears its scaly skin. Underneath it's sort of gray. More stabs. It turns onto its back. It rolls up into a ball. It twists. It gives off a strong smell. It's still trembling a little. We stab some more. Its body goes limp. It doesn't move anymore. That makes one Boche out of the way.

—Traitors like that, they should be shot at once, says the big man of the house.

The radio's on.

It's a lady who's talking.

The big man of the house makes like he's listening, but I know that he does not understand what the lady on the radio is saying.

He drinks the wine in his glass at one go.

—You'd just had a glass, says the skinny little woman.

The big man of the house sits up in his chair.

—Maybe so, but it gets to me, listening to that sort of stuff.

His eyebrows with a lot of hair in them draw closer together.

—People like that deserve a dozen bullets in the gut.

He serves himself another glass of wine.

—Quit drinking, says the skinny little woman. Having one glass more or one glass less won't change anything. There isn't a single thing to be done, is there?

—The single thing to be done is to understand it's because of bastards like that that France is at war.

The skinny little woman is doing her ironing.

—To begin with, who is he, the one talking now?

—Who the hell knows?

The big man of the house bangs his hand down on the table.

—But if it's me, I grab him and *whappo!* Twelve bullets in the gut.

This isn't the first evening the big man of the house is heated up about *that traitor Ferdonnet.*

That traitor Ferdonnet is somebody who talks on the radio and who says that Daladier is a man who has sold himself.

That the French politicians are men who have sold themselves.

That if they hadn't sold themselves the war wouldn't have happened.

That *democracy* is a kind of government that the *Yids* got us.

(The big man of the house doesn't know what the *Yids* are. Neither does the skinny little woman. Neither do the neighbors. Neither do my friends from school. His Reverence says that that hasn't anything to do with us, but that they aren't people like us and that it's wiser not to go around with them.)

That traitor Ferdonnet says that Hitler is going to save Europe.

That traitor Ferdonnet wants France to be with Hitler.

He says that France and Germany are two great countries which ought to get together and not make war on each other.

That the ones who want the war are the politicians and the *Yids*.

That England is run by the *Yids*.

That the English give their machines, and the French their bodies.

(The big man of the house agrees about the English. He says one mustn't count on them too much.)

That traitor Ferdonnet says that the German army is the strongest in the world and that the French soldiers should desert before being crushed by the might of the German army.

That traitor Ferdonnet is a Frenchman who has gone over to Hitler's side.

—I wouldn't want to be his mother, says the skinny little woman.

The neighbors have come over for a little something before supper. There's the smell of anise in the kitchen. I like that yellow smell. The butcher from next door has a knit cap of black wool. There is a woolen pompon at the top. I'd like to burn up that pompon. His wife is pink. Round and pink. They have a son that the guys and I shut up in the cellar for the fun of it. I lead him to the end of the corridor in the dark. He's scared. I pretend I'm a ghost. He lets out a scream. They come downstairs to get us. I get bawled out. I have to sit on a chair and stay put. When there are people at the house I am supposed to be polite. The pink woman takes her child on her lap. She rocks him. He closes his eyes. The drinks are green inside the tall glasses. What's in them is transparent. I ask the big man of the house if I can have a taste. Just with the tip of your tongue, he says. He touches the glass to my lips. I suck in as much as I can. It has a greenish taste, like its color. It's strong and it has a greenish taste.

—He likes it, the little rascal!

That makes everybody laugh.

—Did you see how easy it went down?

I wipe my lips with the back of my hand.

—There's the makings of a real man!

It's strong. It has a green taste and it stays afterward in your nose. I press my tongue against the roof of my mouth. The odor comes back. It's good. The butcher says he would like to join up. His wife says he is too old to volunteer. The butcher says you are never too old to volunteer. His wife says that in a way he is mobilized in his business as a butcher. People have got to eat. Not everybody knows how to cut meat. Say the troops happened to come through the village, there'd have to be meat. The butcher says he is ready. That he will rise to the occasion. The big man of the house refills the glasses. The skinny little woman and the pink woman don't want any more. One glass is enough. They'd start to get tipsy and this is no time for that.

—Ah, women, says the butcher.

—All the same, says the big man of the house.

I have a fart wanting to come out. I hold back. It would make me too ashamed in front of everybody. The big man of the house is farting. I heard him fart several times. I've never heard the skinny little woman. Do all people fart?

—It's the Communists we should have got rid of.

—The Communists, nothing worse than that breed.

They touch glasses for the second time.

—Communists, there's a question they understand, Hitler and his gang. In Germany there're no more Communists. Bye-bye, all gone.

—There's also some who came to this country.

—It's always the same thing, the scum from other countries, we take it right into ours.

The glasses are gradually emptied. They're not for Hitler, but on Hitler's side it isn't all bad either. In his country, he built roads. If that's how you get around in a country, roads matter. Mussolini has also done good things in his country. He's built roads too. And drained the marshes. Naturally, Mussolini's no Hitler. In the Italian army they're all scared. If we have to fight it will be with the Boches. The thing to do is attack right away. That's the butcher's idea. With *the Maginot Line*, there's no way the Boches can get into France. We're well barricaded. We have nothing to worry about. Except that we should have continued *the Maginot Line* along the border with Belgium, says the big man of the house. Up there, where the Belgians are, they can get through. The butcher says we couldn't continue *the Maginot Line* because the Belgians are allies of ours and that might have irritated them, but there isn't any risk because it's made us mass one hell of a lot of troops in that area. The big man of the house says we should have even so. They have their *Siegfried Line* running the whole way, don't they. Their *Siegfried Line*, there's no comparison with *the Maginot*

Line. The butcher says that above all we mustn't wait, that we must attack. Produce *the effect of surprise.* Moreover, they said so over the radio the other day. *The effect of surprise,* and we punch right through them. A week later and we're in Berlin. So strike up the band and forward march! The pink woman says that on the radio they said that, but the butcher doesn't let her finish, he's attacking to the east. Strike up the band! The attack's launched before winter because afterward, with the snow, it'll be too late. That's snow country over there. And once in Berlin that's when we rope that traitor Ferdonnet and put him in the same sack along with Hitler and Goringue. The big man of the house approves of that. The skinny little woman and the pink woman likewise.

It is seven o'clock in the morning. It is cold weather. Since yesterday we are back to wearing sweaters and gloves. The livestock has been brought in from the fields. At the end of the day it snowed a little yesterday. Snowflakes. The big man of the house says that if that had gone on all night we'd have had quite a layer. It's gray. We watch the three buses come up the road. Never do you see them come one after another. The red buses and the blue buses, you see them every day. You only see the yellow buses when the red ones and the blue ones have something the matter with them. There they are, all three. It looks like they're going to drive through the village. They slow down halfway up the hill and turn to get to the square. They move very slowly. We run after them. They stop in front of the big school. It's a building of tired-looking stone. The windows are framed by bricks. It's still empty. The buses park one behind the other. On their roofs are hundreds of suitcases. Packages. Parcels. Sacks. Rolled-up blankets. There are two or three trunks on top of each bus. Red and yellow trunks with initials painted in gold. The doors of the buses open. We're right there in front. Wearing a brown shawl around her shoulders, an old woman is having trouble getting down from the running board. She stumbles. She falls. She remains on the ground. The first driver to climb out helps her up. The gravel has blood on it. The old lady's lip is split open. She says something in a language you don't understand. The driver leans her up against the side of the bus. She is trembling. She is crying. She is bleeding. Her shawl slides down off her shoulders. Nobody dares to pick it up. She has her eyes shut. Eyes stuck way back in the eyeholes. She is crying. A girl wearing a purple dress puts her shawl around her neck. She kisses her hand. She dabs at her mouth. In the bus there are only old men and old women. The old men have canes and hats. Black hats with narrow brims. They have colored strings tied to the collar of their shirts. With the old men and the old women there's only that girl, who's taking care of the old lady who's bleeding, and a tall young man hunched up inside a large and long blue overcoat. His face is white. His eyes are shining. We look at each other and stay that way. That pale thin face stirs something in my heart. His dark eyes fill up mine. He is staring at me. It's as if we'd known each other for a long time. I understand that his face *cannot smile anymore*. He has a lot of black hair.

Inside the blue coat which comes down to his feet his legs are like stilts. He walks the way you walk with stilts. The driver and the old men are busy with the baggage. They pile it against the low wall in front of the school. They move quickly. They aren't saying anything. An old man slumps down over the wall. His arms alongside his body. He is tired. Old women are crying. The girl has led the bleeding one aside. They are on the edge of the road. The girl smiles at me. The old woman is holding a reddened handkerchief in front of her mouth. The girl says something to me in her language. I'm scared. She is nice looking, still I'm scared. I put both hands in front of my crotch and through the cloth grab hold of what's inside. The girl lets out a shriek. The old men and the old women and the young man in the blue coat are sitting in a row on the low wall. Shoulders hunched. It's cold. Some words spoken in a low voice. The village's men have come to see. Some women stop on their way back from their shopping. A car belonging to the gendarmerie. There's a pair of gendarmes. Both of them short and fat. Seeing them, the old men and the old women stand up. The old men take off their hats. The young man with the blue coat remains sitting. He looks like a ghost.

—They're refugees, one gendarme says.

The men nod.

—They're from Alsace, says the gendarme. We're going to put them up in the old school. I'm waiting for the mayor. At the town hall they told us he was in the fields. Us, we can't do anything without him.

—Looks like they're about to fold up.

—It's a way from here, Alsace.

—Maybe they're hungry?

—It's arranged for at noontime, says the gendarme. The mayor said he was taking care of the eats.

The young man in the blue coat growls something sounding like *chichtrak*.

—What's he saying?

—We don't know Alsatian, says the gendarme.

—If they're Alsatians, they're almost Boches?

The gendarme does not reply.

—In German *chichtrak* means shit, a schoolmate says.

We all run off, singing up and down the village streets.

—The *chichtraks* have come! The *chichtraks* have come!

The edges of the river are frozen.

Underneath the little bridge you see a big dark blob.

A schoolmate says it's somebody drowned.

I have already seen drowned people. That's not how they look. Not like a sack.

To make sure you have to get into the water.

The water is ice cold. Not deep but ice cold.

One of the guys goes in. He's taken off his galoshes and his socks.

He says jeez it's cold.

We tell him go on ahead now that you're in there.

He shuffles forward in the water and balances with his arms. When he gets to the dark sack he says it's a jacket.

A man's jacket swollen up with water.

He's told to pull on it.

He pulls on it.

He says that with the man's jacket there's a big white belly.

He's asked what it's a white belly of.

He says it looks like a pig's belly.

Some strange-looking men are crossing over the bridge.

It's the first time we see *uniforms*.

Khaki uniforms.

The men are wearing helmets.

Each has two knapsacks on his back. Crossed straps over his chest.

His rifle on his shoulder.

They say what are you twerps doing around here. You in the water, all you're going to do is freeze to death.

Our guy from school makes it up the bank in a hurry.

We take off across the steeply rising meadows.

Once at the top we turn and look back.

The soldiers in khaki have disappeared.

Then it's the knoll with the gray stones.

Between two stones a rat with its guts hanging out.

Now the guy notices that he forgot one of his socks beside the river.

He says he doesn't care.

The tips of your fingers hurt from the cold.

We reach the shortcut.

The guy says that what he saw in the water was a dead Boche.

At the house I tell the skinny little woman that underneath the bridge we saw a dead Boche.

She says that all I do is tell lies. That I'll have to confess to His Reverence.

That night I dream.

The river is full of dead Boches.

In a street I meet the young man with the blue coat. He reaches out toward me. Reaches out his large white hand. I take off. Then, after I have got away, I turn around. I shout at him:

—*Chichtrak!*

He pitches a stone at me.

Every afternoon at five o'clock the skinny little woman and the other women from the village go to the church to recite twelve prayers for France's victory.

At the church guild they had a missionary

> a missionary is someone like a reverence who is in the colonies to *evangelize* the blacks because the blacks who are not Christians don't have a soul as long as the missionaries haven't *evangelized* them the missionaries give their lives to *evangelize* the blacks and we ourselves in our evening prayers should pray for the *evangelizing* of the blacks and for the aiding of the missionaries

he has a long white beard and he's all dressed in white with a big leather belt around his waist and big sandals with his feet bare inside them and yet it's beginning to get really cold we all have woolen socks on inside our galoshes

> we have been taught that God doesn't like children who turn into mollycoddles that in life you must be of stout heart that Jesus was stout of heart and that he doesn't like children with no backbone

he smiles all the time he looks like he's very nice he handed out candies to us he's the Father we like him a lot he has us play soccer in the courtyard and after when we stop he has us gather around him and he tells us that France is the land of the mighty lords of olden days

> the lords had castles like for example the ruined castle on the heights they used to defend their peasants against those who wished to attack them they were very close friends with the king of France because the king of France was a lord like themselves but a still greater one since he was the king of France

those who built

> he says *raised*

our splendid castles he would like us to be the children of those noble lords he tells us about the Crusades of times bygone

> the Crusades it's when they had to go and win back the tomb of Jesus that lay in *heretic* terri-tory *heretic* is the word for those who do not believe that Jesus came into the world to save mankind and above all our France that we must love with all our heart

he tells us that today it's exactly the same we have to understand and say to our families that France is once again on a crusade against the enemies of God

the enemies of God are the ones called the Reds he says that there are some everywhere even in the village perhaps even in our own family that one can't always recognize them but that it's useful to know it so as to listen only to the word of God whom the Reds want to hurt

he says there is a country that used to be a great country with great emperors and which is run now by the Reds

the Reds that's the Demon the Red Demon it's a Demon which gives pain to the Virgin the angels and all the saints and even our dead would rise up out of their graves if they could to fight against this Red Demon that would like to bring Evil unto the earth

he says that we must take care to remember the name of this Red Demon

the name of this Red Demon is the *Communists*

—Have you heard anything from yours?

—No. How about you?

—We haven't either.

—I'd say it's pretty sloppy the way they've got this thing organized. They take them away from us and we don't even know where they've been put.

—Animals get better treatment.

—And anyhow, the Germans, they haven't done anything to us.

—Ah, poor dearie, if mothers like us only had our say . . .

—But, you know, taking that approach isn't going to do anything for our boys' morale.

—And if they have none at all, where is it all heading?

—It's the government that ought to do something.

—What the government ought to have started by doing is not making war in the first place.

—Making war isn't what we want to do, the people around here.

—No, I don't know many who feel the other way.

—They told me at the town hall that all you put down is the name and somewhere in France for the address.

—What in the world does that mean?

—As if anything could reach him with just that!

—And who wants to waste what goes into the package just to have it wind up lost somewhere.

—Especially because we're in winter and you're going to have to send things to keep warm with.

—Especially because my husband says that in the east it's nippy right now.

—It's downright shameful that we don't even know where they are.

—The ones at the top, they can just straighten the mess out with the Boches their own selves.

—My neighbor even says that her husband knew a Boche some time back, no different from us, willing to help and everything.

—There're good people everywhere.

—In a war it's just the little people who take the beating. They get hurt, the others get the salaries.

—At our place, with my husband and my brother-in-law, we were about ready to hide our lad so he wouldn't go off, but he said he didn't want to do something without the others, they've got their self-respect, you know how it is.

—We ought to have hidden them, all of us.

—My husband says they send the gendarmes.

—The gendarmes! Your Poché fellow, your Glingot! That'd be something to behold!

—Just the two of them, they couldn't do much, you're right.

—My husband says that with the common people in different countries united at last, it isn't in order that we all go and kill each other.

It's known that the Pradiers' son has deserted. (Those Pradiers have always been a hotheaded bunch.)

It's a tan-colored sort of postal card.

Where the stamp should be there's a M.F.

The big man of the house says *military frank*.

That means that the soldier off at war can write home without having to pay for a postage stamp.

Then the skinny little woman asks who does the paying.

The big man of the house says the Post Office does.

The skinny little woman asks the Post Office where? The one the letter is sent from or the one where it is sent to?

The Post Office period. And now leave me alone I've things to do.

It's a card from Uncle Marcel.

He says that everything is all right, that everybody's getting along fine, that they have wine to keep warm with, that so far they haven't seen a single Boche, that if things continue like that he won't complain, he gives everybody in the family a hug, he asks whether maybe we could send him some things to eat, otherwise everything's OK, he sends everybody a hug.

That does something to me says the skinny little woman.

She is holding the card between her fingers as if it were something extraordinary.

You can see that their morale's pretty good says the big man of the house.

The skinny little woman says that we can send him some of the rabbit pâté she made last summer.

And some goat cheese says the big man of the house.

I've knit some socks for him says the skinny little woman.

It's not socks he's asking for says the big man of the house it's stuff to eat with his friends. Eating, food, that kind of thing matters out there. The chow isn't always that great.

I'll put in some rillettes too says the skinny little woman.

The young man with the blue coat is sitting on the wall. He is crying.

The Parisienne is a tall and slender young woman, elegant looking in a colorful loose-fitting dress, she has a hat with a dark little veil attached, with one finger she lifts her veil to slip the cigarette holder between her lips, a long gold cigarette holder, made of gold amber and ivory, the big man of the house says of gold, admiring it, the skinny little woman didn't even know that cigarette holders existed, she thought you smoked the way the big man of the house and the other men in the neighborhood all smoked, now she knows that in Paris you don't smoke the way they do elsewhere, as regards the gold she finds that must be expensive, as regards the amber and the ivory she doesn't know what those things are, the Parisienne wears perfume, she has long red fingernails, big red lips, long red hair, eyes with dark lines around them, she has a pearl necklace which hangs down on her chest and another one made of a mixture of things which sparkles when she moves, when she waves her arm in the air so as to explain that in Germany, in Berlin, Hitler lives in a huge *fabulously* luxurious palace, more luxurious than anything you could even try to imagine in France, he's got so much wealth surrounding him, the big man of the house listens with his mouth open, the skinny little woman shakes her head as if she was saying it's unbelievable anyone could live in such luxury, I listen from over where I'm sitting, I'm sitting on top of the coal box with my legs dangling, I've got something at the end of my foot that hurts, I did nothing but walk all day long, the Parisienne as I look at her looks to me like she isn't real, that big dress she has on and those big necklaces wiggling all the time, those arms waving, that deep-down voice she has, those loud laughs of hers resounding in the kitchen, and above all the cigarette holder in gold and in all the rest, tomorrow I'll tell the whole thing to the guys, Hitler living in a palace, there are white beds covered with skins of animals, because Hitler is a hunter, he kills animals the way he kills humans, he has soldiers along with him who haul out all the animals he kills while hunting and who haul them back to the palace, they make skins you lay on the floor and on the white beds, the Parisienne blows jets of smoke out of her nose, she has a big nose kind of hooked at the end, she says she's not going to worry about fancy manners, we're in the country here among straightforward people, she's going to tuck her veil up out of the way so she can be more comfortable smoking, she offers the big man of the house a cigarette, it's a cigarette with a golden tip, *Oriental* tobacco, the Parisienne gets her cigarettes sent to her from an *Oriental* country, she wonders if they're going to keep on sending them to her in spite of the war, it's a special mixture of three tobaccos, it smells disgusting in the kitchen, the big man of the house says no thanks, he's used to shag, he's sticking to shag, the Parisienne hops up and down on her chair in delight, she didn't know that that's what they called the big man of the house's tobacco, shag, shag, shag, she says it several times over and says that in the country life is extraordinary, she could never do without Paris, but in the country she just goes out of her mind, she wants the big man of the house to roll her a cigarette out of shag,

Hitler doesn't smoke, he doesn't drink, he's a strong man, that's where his strength is, the Boches're rough and tough, strong willed, that's where they get their strength, Hitler's got hundreds of carpets in his palace, but he knows how to make a man cry like a baby, even a soldier, the Parisienne has friends who visited Hitler in his palace, it's more wonderful than anything you can imagine, can you put a cigarette made of shag in this cigarette holder, because without a cigarette holder the smoke makes her cough, the big man of the house is very careful handling the cigarette holder in gold, the skinny little woman says that it's going to be time for supper pretty soon, that if the Parisienne wants to have a bite with them they'll put an extra plate on the table, no problem, the Parisienne likes the idea, what she wouldn't mind having is an omelette country style, an omelette with savory, *aux herbes,* that sort, it's my big toe that's hurting, the toenail must be too long, I have fast-growing toenails, I'll trim it tonight when I'm in bed, there's no savory at this time of year, maybe some cut up onions, the Parisienne loves onion omelettes, with lots of onions, a nice wet runny omelette, you can't find that anymore except in the country, her sister-in-law, the one that's due to arrive tomorrow, she married an officer in the navy, her sister-in-law and her husband received a letter from Hitler, they have a standing invitation to come whenever they want to the *Führer's* place, the skinny little woman gives the big man of the house a questioning look and he pretends not to see it, the Parisienne asks whether they know what the *Führer* is, I curl up my big toes inside my galoshes, the

Führer is the leader, the head, the supreme head of the *Reich,* it hurts down there and itches and I can't scratch where it itches, the *Reich* is Germany, Greater Germany, the *Führer's* Greater Germany, it doesn't matter what France does, when you know the *Reich* and the *Führer,* there are no further questions you need to ask, you know France is beaten in advance, the Parisienne is for the *Führer,* she's not ashamed to say it, besides everything that comes to us from Germany is *prodigious, grandiose,* Wagner, the musician Wagner, *Parsifal, Lohengrin, Bayreuth,* the big man of the house and the skinny little woman don't dare look at each other now, I listen to all those names I can't get a hold on, never have I seen anybody like the Parisienne, she's smoking shag and she's saying by jingo by God there's nothing in this stuff that scares her at all, she'll buy a package of it and she'll have her woman friends in Paris try it out, all of them together they want to buy a house in the country while waiting for things to settle down, but Hitler is a charming man, authoritarian, but charming, for that matter he's crazy about women, he has one every evening in his palace and he's more fun than a barrel of monkeys, that's what they say, that sets the Parisienne to laughing.

What they say is that the garage mechanic is a *Communist.*

—You know what they are, your Alsatians there? asks the rural police officer.

He's talking to two men and a woman.

—They're Boches?

—They aren't Boches says the rural police officer.

The two men and the woman wait for the explanation.

—Your Alsatians, they're Jews.

They think about that.

One of the men asks, Jews? What's that?

The rural police officer rubs his hands together and hunches up his shoulders.

—They're Jews. That's all I've been told.

The woman says, So? Does that change something?

The fish-and-game warden doesn't know.

—Well, in a way, sure. If they're Jews they stop being Alsatians.

—Where do they come from then? one of the men asks.

The rural police officer doesn't know.

—They come from where they come from, but all you can say is that the likes of them don't much fit with the likes of the people from around here.

—That's the truth, the woman says.

—True enough, says one of the men.

The rural police officer takes the three of them to witness.

—We were minding our own business here, where we belong, and then all of a sudden they start arriving from all sides.

—That's the truth, the woman says.

—True enough, says one of the men.

The rural police officer is aware of what's been going on.

—With them they have a tall young fellow, you know the one I mean?

The woman says, You see him everywhere with that blue coat of his.

One of the men says, He's all the time running up and down the streets.

—Well, the rural police officer says, well last night he broke around thirty windows at the school.

—Thing to do then is just give it to him good, says one of the men.

The rural police officer agrees.

—That one! He's a mean son of a bitch!

—Thing to do is send him back where he came from, says one of the men.

The woman says, No one goes and breaks their windows!

—I'm not fighting a war for the millionaires, the garage mechanic says one day.

—We've got to lower the boom on fascism, the garage mechanic says another day.

—This war and us workers—the two don't go together, the garage mechanic says one day.

—Proletarians have to stand together and arm themselves against fascism, the garage mechanic says another day.

Fascism, proletarians, the skinny little woman asks what those words mean.

The big man of the house says he'll explain to her later.

Later, the big man of the house says the proletarians will win out over fascism.

—You've been off again having a glass before supper with the garage mechanic, says the skinny little woman.

The big man of the house says he has a glass before supper with whoever he damned well pleases.

—Even with Communists? the skinny little woman comes back sharply.

The big man of the house says that the Communists may not be wrong about everything.

The skinny little woman says that that does it.

—And to begin with, the two of you, it's not one glass you put away, it's three or four.

The big man of the house says that there's war and that men have got to discuss with each other.

The skinny little woman says that if there wasn't anybody but them to save France the country would be in a pretty mess all right.

They sing "We're Going to Hang Out Our Wash on the Siegfried Line." The Maginot Line and the Siegfried Line, I don't understand what either of them is. How I see them is like lines you draw in the exercise book with your fifteen-centimeter wooden ruler with the brass edge. The inventor of the Maginot Line is Monsieur Maginot. He's an *engineer*. I don't understand what is meant by going to hang our wash out on the Siegfried Line. One morning I see the skinny little woman putting the wash out on the wire in the garden. The Siegfried

Line is a wire. Do soldiers in the war have to do their wash? On the village square the kids pretend they're soldiers. They march in step, they salute, they sing "We're Going to Hang Out Our Wash on the Siegfried Line" as loud as they can. People give them pennies and pieces of candy. I think it's a stupid song. They sing "Bolleros y mantillas." You make your tongue vibrate in your mouth and between your teeth so that your *r*'s will roll a lot. You do like the *singer*. She's a Spanish singer. Her name is Rina Ketty. There's a picture of her on the paper of the song. First you hear her on the radio and then you buy the little paper where they have the words and the music with the picture of Rina Ketty or the picture of the man or the woman singer who's singing the song. Rina Ketty is beautiful. She has beautiful dark eyes. What you like is her *burning* voice, it's the garage mechanic who said that, the big man of the house agrees, he too says that Rina Ketty has a *burning* voice. What I especially like is her way of rolling her *r*'s. When I'm out in the street by myself, with my hands in my pockets, I try to roll my *r*'s a lot. There are some kids who aren't able to. I am also very good at whistling. I'd really like to be a singer and have my picture on the little paper. There're photos in blue, in red, or in brown. I'd sing on the radio and they'd say I'm good at rolling my *r*'s. Sometimes I am a singer like Rina Ketty, but I can also be the President of the Republic, Albert Lebrun. I don't understand why everybody calls him *Albert Twinkletoes*. I can also be General Gamelin. He is at the head of the troops in the war. I can also be Adolf Hitler in my big palace full of rugs with women. I haven't seen as many pictures of him, that makes it less easy. I am an airplane pilot. Or I drive a tank. I arrive in the village with my tank. I drive around the streets. I squash anything ahead of me that gets in my way. Tanks will squash anything. People watch my tank go by. They are afraid to let out a peep. I drive off. Nobody knew that inside the tank it was me. The next day my friends tell me what happened. They're singing "Le plus beau de tous les tangos du monde." That's Tino Rossi. I'm good at imitating him. If there are visitors at the house they ask me to imitate him. I am sure of hearing them clap at the end. They say you'd say it's Tino. "We're Going to Hang Out Our Wash on the Siegfried Line," we sing that too.

The young man with the blue overcoat goes around the streets shouting. He is tall. He is stooped over. He is pale. He has sad eyes. He has a hoarse voice, dried out. As if he had a lot of flour in his mouth. He shouts in French that he is Jewish. He's frightening. I feel sorry for him. I'd like to be like him. I'd like to have his big blue overcoat. I'd like to have his long legs. I'd like to be stooped over. I'd like to be pale and to have sad eyes. Me too, I'd shout that I was Jewish. At night when I'm saying my prayers I often think about him. I think about him so much that I stop thinking about God. At night sometimes when I am too sleepy as you sometimes are when you're saying your prayers I get to believing that he and the little Jesus are the same thing. The next day, the young man in the blue overcoat, there he is again.

He frightens me more than ever. There are some guys who say that the Jews are the ones who put Jesus on the cross and that it's on account of that that you shouldn't like them. The young man in the blue overcoat magnetizes me. I follow him at a distance the whole afternoon. He doesn't stop walking with his long legs and his big blue overcoat. While he walks he talks to himself. He waves his arms. He throws himself onto the ground. He hammers with his fists. He cries out. He is unhappy. What I can tell is that when you are Jewish you are unhappy. You have a big blue overcoat. You are pale. You have sad eyes. You are unhappy. If he notices I am following him he gets angry. He spits. He says things in Alsatian. I make faces at him. I put my hand on my sex. I turn my behind toward him and point to it. I yell *chichtrak!* at him.

It's barely daylight.

Out on the road you hear horses' hooves.

We go and look out the window.

There's a column of horses with peasants walking next to them each with a stick in his hand.

The big man of the house says holy God.

His eyes are moist.

The skinny little woman says there's something she prefers not to look at.

The air is blurry from mist.

On the square there are horses all over.

Tethered horses.

Horses that are loose.

They sniff at the dust.

They snort.

They whinny.

More horses arrive from down below and come down from up above.

With peasants.

Everybody's cold.

I'm cold.

Do the horses feel cold?

The peasants are talking to their horses.

The peasants stroke their horses and pat them.

The horses nuzzle their heads against them.

The horses whinny.

As if they were crying.

More horses are arriving from everywhere.

There's clattering on the pavement.

On the road, the sound of hooves in the dirt.

The peasants have their jaws clenched.

The peasants are caressing their horses, rubbing their horses' noses.

There's one peasant who's crying.

There's another peasant who's also crying.

They turn their heads away so they won't be seen crying.

The big man of the house has come over.

He's holding me by the hand.

He says holy God, I never would have believed I'd see such a thing.

He wipes his eyes and his mustache with his hand.

My hand is little inside his.

He knows some peasants.

They say hello to each other.

No one wants to talk.

The horses piss.

The horses make their dung.

The horses scrape their hooves.

Everybody's cold.

My gut feels cold inside.

All these horses on the square.

All these peasants not speaking.

A horse lies down.

Its peasant hunkers down beside it.

Its peasant lays his hand on its head.

The last horses are arriving.

The square is filled with horses.

It smells of horses.

There are horses that have feed bags made of dark cloth.

There are horses that have several colors.

There is a small horse.

The peasant has his hand on its neck.

The horse laughs, showing its big teeth.

You hear nothing but the noise coming from the horses.

Monsieur the Collector of Revenues arrives on his horse.

His horse is slender and delicate next to the others.

His horse has long legs spotted with white.

Holy God, now don't tell me they're going to take that one too, says the big man of the house.

Monsieur the Collector of Revenues salutes everybody like a soldier.

The peasants take off their hats.

Monsieur the Collector of Revenues says that if they take his horse from him he'll kill it right there and after that he'll kill himself.

He lifts the flap of his jacket and pulls a revolver from the holster on his belt.

Holy God says the big man of the house.

The peasants lower their heads.

You feel the anger.

You feel the gloom.

You feel the hate.

Great God almighty.

The big man of the house has a terrible look on his face.

The car drives up.

In it there's a sergeant and three soldiers.

The soldiers look ashamed of themselves.

The horses whinny.

The peasants press their bodies up against the bodies of their horses.

The sergeant is in a tight corner.

He's in a tight corner says the big man of the house.

I have a chill in my stomach.

I think I'm going to be sick.

One of the soldiers goes around with the sergeant.

The soldier lifts the horse's upper lip to see its teeth.

The sergeant looks at the teeth.

He says good for service.

The peasant wraps his arms around his horse's neck and kisses its nose.

Motionless in his saddle Monsieur the Collector of

Revenues repeats to the sergeant what he said earlier.

The sergeant orders him to get down off his horse.

Monsieur the Collector of Revenues refuses.

He forbids them to touch the mouth of his horse.

The sergeant orders the soldier to lift up the horse's lip.

Monsieur the Collector of Revenues says be careful I'll put a bullet through your head.

Holy God says the big man of the house.

The sergeant says all right all right we'll attend to this later.

Monsieur the Collector of Revenues puts his revolver away, says to the peasants I'm with you, and he turns his horse around and rides away.

We ought to all do like him a peasant says in a strong voice.

Oh I don't think I'd advise that says the sergeant.

The horse vans arrive.

That frightens the horses.

They smell death says the big man of the house.

I hear it was dreadful, that requisition, the skinny little woman says at midday while serving the oven-baked potatoes.

It's snowing. It snowed the whole night. Our soldiers are going to be cold.

It's snowing.

The radio says that the *atmospheric conditions* (the *atmospheric conditions*, that's the kind of weather it is) are interrupting all our troops' activity.

That *solidarity* is necessary between us and our soldiers who are shivering in the trenches (*solidarity* is when you think about others).

It's snowing.

It's the *drôle de guerre* (the *drôle de guerre* is when the soldiers aren't fighting).

—God almighty, back then, in '14, they didn't look to see if it was snowing or not. Every day was good weather for blowing us to hell.

—It isn't the same war anymore, says the skinny little woman.

—No, it isn't the same war anymore, that's obvious. If they're waiting now for summer in order to fight, this war's liable to last for some time.

—So long as it's this way, says the skinny little woman, at least you're sure there aren't any dead or wounded.

—And the Boches? asks the big man of the house. How we're going to mop the floor with them?

—You, you're always wanting to mop the floor with everybody, says the skinny little woman.

—If you're fighting a war it's for some purpose, and if not then there's no point in it, says the big man of the house.

—Whatever, it'll get itself fought soon enough, this war of yours, says the skinny little woman.

—That's just what the garage mechanic was saying to me only yesterday, it's the war of the big boys who eat the money, says the big man of the house.

It's snowing.

This afternoon I'm going to go sledding with the guys.

The Parisienne is walking back and forth inside the house. She is in her *kimono*. (A *kimono* is like a dressing gown, but split up along the legs.) On the stairs you see her thighs. She has her thighs bare or with stockings on. The garage mechanic says to the big man of the house you hit the jackpot. The skinny little woman says it isn't thinkable for a woman to walk around like that. The big man of the house says that she's a Parisienne. The garage mechanic tells the big man of the house he wouldn't mind *having himself a piece* of that. (I know what that means. Me too, I wouldn't mind *having myself a piece* of the Parisienne.) She appears unexpectedly in the kitchen while the skinny little woman is at her sewing machine in front of the window. The Parisienne sits down, making herself comfortable. She talks about the war. She has a *lover* at the front. (*Lover* is the person who *has himself a piece* of the Parisienne.) She has packages sent to him with the very best of all sorts of food and clothing. He tells her in a card (she gets the card out of her handbag, a big handbag, maybe tiger skin) that he and some other officers have been discussing the situation and that it's *Heil Hitler.* (*Heil,* that means greetings and good health to the Führer. You stretch out your arm in front of the Führer and you say *Heil* in a loud voice.) It's a code she and her *lover* have together. *Heil Hitler* means everything's going well. The Parisienne would like to go to the front. She would also like to go to Berlin and see Hitler. She'd stretch out her arm, she'd say *Heil Hitler,* and she would talk with him about Beethoven and Wagner. She is sure that Hitler would understand that in

France there are people like her and like her friends in Paris who are *pro-German*. (The garage mechanic looked that up in the dictionary. It means being for the Germans.) She has her legs crossed so high up that you see the bottom part of her rear end. The other day going up the stairs she stuck her hand between my legs.

Off at the war there's
Uncle Emile
Uncle Marcel
Uncle Alfred
Céline's son
Henri
and André's son.

The chow's all right. There's better, but there's worse. You see the Boches over on the other side. Until now not one shot has been fired from a rifle. From time to time the artillery pops away. In the sky you mainly see Boche aircraft. The officers, it's the same as everywhere. You've got mean bastards and you've got good guys. So far we've been doing pretty good. All we're really short on is there's not enough wine. The guys get together after supper and that leaves a bunch of empty bottles. You're reminded of the good old days. Except for the tail, that's all that's missing. When we show up on leave, look out. You just tell the girls that all they need to do is hold on. We've got pictures hung up. We were worried there'd be cooties. Aren't any cooties. The adjutant goes around doing the disinfection. With a little more wine and a little more you know what there'd be nothing to object to. It's the *drôle de guerre*. Funny sort of war, all right.

The great big character with the military hat, the uniform and the *Sam Browne belt* (it's a belt that comes down across your chest) is Hitler. He's attached to the pole on the square, he's quietly swaying, he has his legs apart, they've given him a big mustache and a lick of hair which comes out from under the hat, the whole village is standing around the pole and laughing, some are saying that they ought to have pulled his pecker out, Adolf's pecker, he has a huge belly, some of us ask what's inside it, we're told it's straw but inside you hear like it was a cat meowing, it's the strongest ones who shinny up the pole with a knife between their teeth to let the air out of Hitler, those who make it up there slash at the dummy a couple of times, that puts holes in the uniform, there are bits of straw coming out, little by little the hole's getting bigger, the thing is to stab in the right place, down below they're whooping it up, straw is blowing around, everybody's yelling and clapping, there'd been a suckling pig in Hitler's stomach, the dummy had been slashed all over, the pig had tumbled out, it's squealing, it tries to run away, it's grabbed, it's given to the winner, he's holding it by the tail, upside down, the pig keeps squealing, Hitler has been brought down, they're dancing on him, he's in pieces now, it's not about to be forgotten, how Hitler gave birth to a pig.

There are birds shivering on the leafless branches.

The refugees were *in transit*. The rural policeman said they were leaving tomorrow. The two gendarmes said the same. According to everyone the refugees were *in transit*. I did not see anything more of the young man with the blue overcoat.

IN TOWN MAMA GUITE IS A DRESSMAKER. SHE SELLS cloth, overalls, and aprons at the outdoor markets. I sleep in a little bed piled up with pieces of cloth with checks and flowers. It is also the place where Mama Guite cuts out the aprons. She sews in the kitchen where she has a big machine which whirs all day long and late into the night. Mama Guite has an automobile. That's rare. On market days she goes to get it from the garage. It's not yet daylight. She parks in front of the house and we load it up with merchandise. We have our coffee. We lock up everywhere and off we go. At the marketplace I help her plant the stakes and put up the awning. It's heavy. Mama Guite teaches me. I sell right alongside her. I do fine. Nothing is like in the country. The people don't know one another. In the street where we live we know only two or three persons. We know the baker, his wife, and his daughter. Our house is not far from the hospital. They say that on account of the hospital we won't get bombed. We are also not far from the airfield. The airfield could catch it. Mama Guite is a woman who is not afraid of anything.

My friends.

—We don't need you.

—You're Spaghetti. The Spaghettis, they're against us in the war.

—The Spaghettis ought to eat their spaghetti in their own country.

—The Dirlo told us anybody who's got a Boche name, a Spaghetti name, or a Jew name, we shouldn't even talk to them.

—We're not talking to you anymore.

—A Jew and a Spaghetti, it's like a Boche. Just the same.

—Maybe he's a Spaghetti and a Jew both?

I start punching.

It's known that we have Jews on our street.

At least four of them.

At the end of the street is a woman married to a Jew.

Jews, they figure out ways not to get called up when there's a war.

Jews, they get wars started between other people.

And it's the Jews who pocket the money.

In the center of the city the windows of Italian shops have been broken with rocks and with hammers.

With Mama Guite we went to have a look.

It's an Italian meat store.

They had swept up the bits of broken glass on the sidewalk.

That made quite a pile.

Spaghettis go home is written on the wall.

With black paint.

In big letters.

In another street it's an Italian cheese shop.

The same thing is written there.

At the cheese shop there were two people hurt.

The owner and his son.

They were hurt by being hit with hammers.

They are in the hospital.

Hey now, how do you like that? They're putting Spaghettis in our hospitals.

All they needed to do was send them back to Mussolini.

Here in France the Spaghettis eat our bread and sleep with our women.

That's all that Spaghettis are good at.

At screwing broads.

A couple of bars on the old mandolin and the broad thinks that this is it.

Can't stand those bastards.

Let them go play their mandolins for Mussolini.

Mama Guite was married to an Italian.

A mason.

He died from tuberculosis at the start of the war.

She takes me by the hand.

We turn around and leave.

At first, she doesn't say anything, but farther on she says that if they come to her house to do that stuff they'll find out who they're messing with.

Mama Guite is a woman who is not afraid of anything.

The workingman next door who is at the military arsenal says that the new prime minister is the one who once referred to the workers as the dirty bastards that wear caps.

Mama Guite knows nothing at all about politics.

I like getting the lowdown on politics.

Why the governments change.

Why it's Paul Reynaud instead of Daladier.

Mama Guite also owns a radio.

I listen to songs.

I listen to what they say about the war.

They say it's all right. That it's the *drôle de guerre*.

Mama Guite has three brothers at the front.

Antoine, Victor, and Loulou.

Hitler is making speeches.

Reynaud is making speeches.

I listen to Tino Rossi and Rina Ketty.

Mama Guite doesn't like songs.

She says that listening to the radio is a waste of time.

She sews day and night.

She has masses said for her husband's soul.

We go to them early in the morning.

Before going to set up at the market.

In the church we're the only ones.

The two of us and one or two old ladies.

The priest says that it is in order that Mama Guite's husband may rest in peace.

Mama Guite cries.

She cries and she prays.

When it is over at the church we go home and then we go to the market.

In a drawer of a little dresser full of different kinds of stuff I found a book.

I'm reading it, and this is the first time I have ever read a real book.

If Mama Guite didn't tell me to turn off the light I would read all night.

In the book it's several stories that aren't connected.
I would enjoy writing a book of my own.

In the pure morning sky. Airplanes zooming
upward. Banking. Diving. Doing tight rolls. Chasing
each other. Now you'd say the motors had quit. Now
they've started back up. There's a lot of bright sun. The
planes dip behind the houses. They skim just above their
roofs. They climb. It's above the airfield. A deep thud in
the sky. Mama Guite is looking up along with me. The
windows are full of people looking up. The sky is a sheet
of blue. The planes gleam. You see their windowpanes.
On the tail some planes have a broken cross. A real black
cross painted on the belly. A neighbor at his window
says to us that they're the Boches. Machine guns going
full blast. Mama Guite asks him what the broken crosses
are. It's the *swastika*. The cross the Boches have. A plane
explodes. Flames shooting out from all sides. A big
cloud of black smoke. He got hit, says the neighbor
standing at his window. You can no longer see any sky.
Only billows of black smoke. I ask Mama Guite if it was
a Boche or a French plane that blew up. She doesn't
know. She says it's the same. The neighbor at his window
says it was a Boche. Above the smoke, planes are still
going at it. You hear the radio this morning the neighbor asks over there at his window. Mama Guite says no.
From the looks of it our troops could be heading for the
showers. In France it's always the same thing, not
enough armor, not enough aircraft. Armor, Mama Guite
tells me, that's tanks. They're for spearheading attacks.
The Boches are attacking from all sides at once says the

neighbor standing at his window. And the Maginot Line asks Mama Guite. The Maginot Line, it can't be expected to take care of everything all by itself says the neighbor at his window. He also says that anyway it was a foregone conclusion that we were going to lose this war. Mama Guite says that her father had been badly wounded in '14 and that she has three brothers at the front. They'll be done with it soon, says the neighbor at his window. The Boches are going to wrap it up in a hurry, it won't take long. They'll call for an armistice. So much the better, says Mama Guite. That way it'll be peace and everybody will return home. That's all everybody is hoping for, says the neighbor at his window. Another airplane explodes inside the black smoke.

The mass is at seven in the morning. Before the elevation of the Host the siren starts up. It's the warning. Bombs are falling. The church windows are trembling. The panic-stricken priest turns around toward Mama Guite and me. He makes the sign of the cross for us. In his other hand he is holding the chalice, covered over with a piece of cloth. Bent in two from fear he scurries off in the direction of the parsonage. Mama Guite can't believe her eyes. The old fart she says. We cross ourselves. We leave the church. The bombs are coming down. We have a way to go. We hurry along the street. Mama Guite runs into someone she knows. He says he's leaving with his children. Says we got to get out. Along the avenue the trees have nice green leaves. There's a blackbird with its yellow beak. The bombs come down. I

78

have a top in my pocket. It's too bad I can't see the bombs. The man we've run into looks about as scared as the curé. The sky is blue. Blue. Blue. It's clear. It's nice and bright. It's nice warm weather. You feel good. The bombs come down. The blackbird with its yellow beak hops around in the gutter. Farther on it's a sparrow. A fat little sparrow. I say *whischt, whischt* at it. It flies away. The air has a caramel taste. Mama Guite is walking fast. I run a little to keep up with her. Mama Guite has her head out there in front, like she was about to ram right through something. She's strong. With her you aren't afraid. I feel like spinning my top. A spinning top, that makes me think that nothing is true. That everything can just fly away. That I could fly away, me too. The bombs come down. Mama Guite is telling me it's all on fire. Above the roofs there's thick smoke. We keep walking. It seems to me there's something rose colored in everything around us. Mama Guite takes hold of my hand. We go into the police station. The sergeant at the desk says Madame don't you realize it's crazy you being out in the street with a child. Mama Guite says that the reason she is is to come and find out just what you're supposed to do. The sergeant says to her Madame if you can leave, then leave. Mama Guite asks when. The police sergeant says to her right away. Defeat he says, we are being defeated. The Germans have entered France. They're advancing as if they were moving through butter. Mama Guite asks where they're at. The police sergeant tells her that no one has any idea. An hour ago they were at one place, an hour later they are somewhere else. There's never been anything like it. Mama Guite says she has three brothers at the front. The desk sergeant tells her there is no more front. It's a rout, helter-skelter everywhere. The French army is beaten. Bombs are falling. Madame says the desk sergeant, just leave. I have a car says Mama Guite. One more reason for leaving. Take the youngster and leave. We run the whole way to the house. We pile everything we can into the car. Bolts of cloth. Sheets. Pillows. Clothing. Shoes. The car is ready to burst. At the last moment Mama Guite tosses her dead husband's photo onto the heap of odds and ends. We climb into the car. We need to get gas. The garage mechanic says you want gas then you better hurry. You'll be the last who gets any. After you I'm pouring what's left down the drain. I have orders not to leave gas for the Boches. We drive across the town. There are lots of people on the sidewalks. With suitcases and with sacks. Some are going in this direction, some are going in the other. We head out toward where Mama Guite's aunt lives in the country. She's never made a trip this long since she's owned her car. There are no more bombs coming down. The all clear hasn't even been sounded. The shops have their steel shutters lowered. We are stopped by two gendarmes. They look at Mama Guite. They look at me. They look inside the car. They ask Mama Guite where she is going. They wave us on. They give a salute when we start off. We cross a bridge over the river. The town is in sunshine, the sky above is blue. The water in the river is green. Far away in the distance you see the clear green of the water. I feel like I'd like to get into the green water. I don't know how to swim. The water is green and the bridge is white. There are gendarmes but they don't say anything to us. The car is too full up says Mama Guite. She says that her dead husband will protect us.

Old women flopped down at the side of the road.
Old women and old men flopped down at the side of the road.
Old suitcases flopped down next to them at the side of the road.
Old women and old men flopped down by the roadside, sobbing.

Men, women, children, old people, horses, donkeys, mules, dogs, cats.
Horses that skid and fall on the road.
Dogs that are scared and that are barking from fear on the road.
The run-over cats on the road.
The blood-covered cats run over on the road.

A lost child who's crying at the side of the road.

A lost child who's bleeding at the side of the road.

Mama Guite says that if she goes on crying at the wheel pretty soon she won't be able to drive anymore.

Men, women, suitcases, animals, jumbled together on the road.

Carts overloaded with children and baggage drawn by a horse that's bucking and rearing in the middle of the crowd.

Older boys on bicycles, heads lowered, pedaling at top speed along the road.

A road packed with people who are walking, people who are crying, people who are in pain, people who are thirsty, people who are asleep on their feet, people who are bent double under what they are carrying, people who are stumbling, people who are falling, people who are being shoved off the road, people being left by the wayside, sick people who are off the road vomiting on the grass.

A child in tears holding its stomach with both hands at the side of the road.

A mother going crazy who's screaming out a name at the side of the road.

Mama Guite is afraid of these hundreds and hundreds of people who are liable to trample us to death.

Men who are fighting for space on the road.

Broken chairs on the road.
A slop pail on the road.
A sack of flour split open on the road.

A broken pair of eyeglasses on the road.

Broken chairs on the road.

An open suitcase spewing its dirty clothes out onto the road.

A dignified-looking girl who is holding two children by the hand on the road.

Bleeding feet on the road.

A man who is eating while he walks on the road.

A horse with a bleeding hoof on the road.

A rolled-up mattress on the road.

A child's pair of shorts on the road.

Mama Guite says we'll never make it with all these poor people swarming the road.

Clothing, shoes, bundles, suitcases, trunks, chests, sacks, packages, knapsacks, satchels, saddlebags, string, wire, straps, crates, blankets, suitcases, trunks, bundles, footlockers, knapsacks, packages, dangling from hands, perched on shoulders, lugged on backs, hung around the waists of children, slung from cords, higgledy-piggledy, right side up and upside down, piled together in haste, grabbed hold of in fear, all sorts of stuff, useful things, superfluous things, parcels, bundles, suitcases.

A man and a woman pushing a baby carriage along the road.

Carts, pushcarts, vehicles big and small, teams, rigs, wheelbarrows.

Loads collapsing, scattering over the road. Pots and pans. Broken dishes. Tinware, forks and spoons. Sheets, towels. A frying pan. A platter for serving snails.

A woman who falls to her knees and begins to pray on the road. She is knocked over. She is trampled. The crowd advances.

Mama Guite says she wants to stop but can't it keeps coming on behind and you have to keep moving otherwise the cars run into you and shove you into the ditch.

Hens, rabbits, chicken coops, rabbit cages.

A fat man who is spitting blood from his mouth.

The army trucks that come from the other direction and drive right into the crowd.

Soldiers who have raised the tarp at the back of the truck and who are yelling get off to the side get off to the side.

Wooden barriers funneling traffic. The piling up. The struggling. The crushing. Cars force their way ahead. Collisions. Dull sounds of impact. Yells.

Torn-apart shoes.

An officer on horseback.

All these men who no longer have any idea where they have come to.

All these women crying.

All these men who no longer have any idea where they're going.

All these women who are holding their children tight in their arms.

Barkings, caterwaulings, creakings, grindings, yellings, poundings, hammerings, groanings, burstings, slammings, cracklings.

An enormous choking stifling suffocation.

Mama Guite says that her dead husband will guide us to the very end.

Upon the road of the white stuff, of the milky stuff, of the floppy stuff, of the shapeless stuff, of the gooey stuff.

Upon the road of blue oil.

Upon the road of blood.

A flow of living beings.

Busted cars.

Bunches of kids no longer accompanied by anybody.

Abandoned cars.

Disorder.

Fear.

Panic.

Fear.

Panic.

Fear.

Panic.

Country of runaways.

Mama Guite's face is streaming with tears.

The country aunt is all by herself in her house. Her husband is at the war. Dispatch rider. She says *displatch*. Her husband is a Communist. Several times he had had run-ins with the gendarmes. He had told the whole village that he wouldn't go to the war. That if the gendarmes came to get him he'd fill their asses with buckshot. The gendarmes are capitalism's watchdogs. Then war had been declared. He had ridden off on his motorcycle. By himself. He refuses to put on a uniform. They took him the way he was. He does his dispatch riding with his motorcycle. Three times he surrendered to the Germans. Three times the Germans took his rifle and told him to go back where he came from. He has returned to his unit. There's been no more news from him. When he comes back from the war he will build a house for his family. He is a master mason. They already have the land. Not far from the road. The country aunt has no news from him but she knows nothing has happened to him. He told her he'd come back, he'll come back. We'll have a bedroom upstairs. The house doesn't have electricity. Light comes from acetylene lamps. We'll have candles to go upstairs and to see in the bedroom. You can still see well enough to be able to sleep. The country aunt has a sister in the Nord who left everything behind, like the rest. She was supposed to come. She hasn't come. With all these people on the highways maybe she has been held up. Or maybe she has taken the wrong road. Her husband too is off at the war. You ask yourself how all these people on the roads are able to get their bearings. Every afternoon the country aunt goes to stand by the edge of the road to watch the people going past. She's seen all sorts. It doesn't stop. Even at night. If it was her, at night she'd be frightened. The younger ones, it's not so bad, but the elderly ones, that gets to you for sure. Going by they look at you with eyes that give you the shivers. The other day there was one who was thirsty. Nobody had any water. Someone went to get some. The time it took to go and come back, by then the poor old man was gone, pushed on by the crowd. If it isn't a shame to see such things. She wonders what her husband would do if he saw that. Him being a Communist. And he wasn't a pretend Communist. He used to share all his earnings with his workers. She knows a gendarme. He told her that when her husband is discharged he'd better be careful. Just the sight of a Communist, it's more than the Boches can stand. Between them you might say there's the difference between night and day. This evening she's going to make some good soup for us and give us some goat cheese.

We're told (somebody says something about something someone else says something else about it everybody repeats what he heard going around)

we're told that if ever there was any danger with the German air force (the German airplanes are called *stukas* they are fast fighter planes faster than the French planes faster than the English planes the German air force is faster than any other people have also noticed that we have hardly any planes up there to face the German air force the German air force is called the *Luftwaffe* the head of the *Luftwaffe* is called Göring he's the one the big man of the house used to call Goringue)

we're told that if ever there was any danger with the German air force the French fighter planes would fly over the village making a siren type of sound (the villagers have never heard any siren and the people on the road don't know that the French planes will give out with a siren)

we went out to see the procession on the road (we recognized somebody from our street who was moving fast on a bicycle he didn't see us)

we came back through the meadows (the sirens of the two airplanes were hard to hear)

we watched the planes which were flying low people

hung around waving in their direction (neither Mama Guite nor the country aunt nor I nor anybody had understood)

we watched them circle three or four times over our heads (the French planes had gone there were flowers in the meadows daisies the floppy-eared dog kept its eyes on them)

we heard the bursts of machine gun fire (it was causing dotted lines in the grass not far from us)

we turned round to look (the German airplanes were already off in the distance)

we saw the dead child (its head blown open).

A man, his wife, his young daughter, each with two big suitcases, they stumble along, clumsy, harassed, their clothes are dirty, he is unshaven, his hair is uncut, their faces are sallow, gaunt, their eyes big and staring, they ask questions to left and to right, have the Germans been seen, in which direction, they don't know the news, they have been walking for such a long time, they are Jewish, the Germans are killing the Jews, they had family in Germany, they don't know what has happened to them, might there be a vacant house in the village, they have some money, a little bit of money, might they be able to stop, two soldiers riding a motorcycle, they say the Boches have shown up in the area, the man, his wife, and his young daughter turn right around, panic-stricken.

A young soldier in rags.
His rifle in his hand.
He moves forward like a robot.

He is bareheaded.

His insignia hang upon his buttonless jacket.

The knees of his pants are torn.

It could be that he has no shirt on.

An old man gives him a glass of wine.

He drinks it all in one gulp.

He says thanks.

He says he lost contact with the others.

He says they've all had enough of this.

He says the war is all horseshit.

He says the first one who gives him any trouble he'll shoot the fucker.

He says they had them fight a war that was lost ahead of time.

He says that what the politicians need is a bayonet in the belly.

He says the same goes for the generals.

He says that France is shit that's what.

He says that he doesn't give a shit.

He says that his buddies are dead.

He says he's going home.

The government has moved to Bordeaux. There isn't any more government in Paris. How can it be that there is no more government in Paris?

—They were scared shitless, that's all, one man said.

A woman has seen the Germans in the adjoining village. They'll be here in a quarter of an hour. Hide the children. Lock the doors and the shutters. Get your provisions into the cellar. They're breaking in everywhere. They ransack everything. They steal everything. They eat everything. They rape the women. They kidnap the children. They catch a child. They throw it beneath the treads of a tank. The child is mashed flat. They carry off the champagne. The soldiers all march with a bottle of champagne in each hand. They have a photo of Hitler on their uniform. They let out horrible yells. They have red ears. They break things for the fun of it. They rip open mattresses. They steal the money. They make off with the silver. They catch a child. They throw it beneath the treads of a tank. The child is mashed flat. Hide the children. Stay indoors. Lock everything.

—Where they died is not known, somewhere outside, their house had been empty for over a week, they had taken their cat, Boulot, they never went anywhere without their cat, it was the mayor's office that notified us, they are all four of them dead, the father, the mother, the two children, where their bodies are is not known, there are procedures that would have to be followed, papers to be filled out, this isn't the suitable moment, and moreover, at this stage, what purpose would it serve?

We gather a big bouquet of field flowers.

The gendarmes bring her her husband's identity disk and his haversack.

In the haversack, held together by a rubber band, are

all the letters she wrote to him from the time the war began.

The country aunt pedals back from her errands on her bicycle. She is proud of having a man's bike. It's her husband's. Before going off to his unit he told her everything she'd have to do in the house while he wasn't there. He would have written it all down for her but she can't read. She was able to memorize everything. For the bike, once a month you have to lubricate the sprocket with a special oil. She doesn't like going on foot to do her errands. She rides all the time. In and around the village they're a familiar sight, her and her bike. She comes back shortly before noon. She says there was a mob with His Honor the mayor and that he said there would soon be restrictions, that is to say nothing like the amount of food available we've got now. It doesn't matter to her. She has her hens, she has rabbits. And the pig. She grows her leeks and her potatoes in a rented patch. In front of the house she's planted her squash. In back are the currant bushes for the jelly. She does not understand why there'd be restrictions. Don't tell me, she says, that the Boches are going to eat everything.

A blue sky, verbena blue.
A mild temperature for the season.
Birds.
Frogs in the pond.
A little girl with blond hair.
A white dress.

Flounces that flutter.

Passages of lace.

Everybody saying what lovely weather.

Everybody saying what a shame there should be this wretched war going on.

Everybody saying it will be over soon.

A sky woven out of blue.

The heat.

Dogs.

Antoine had been in the Maginot Line. He was taken prisoner.

Victor was in the Nord. Near Dunkerque.

Loulou is in Algeria. He was doing his military service there. Then the war broke out.

It is midday. I'm slow returning to the house. (There's this column of ants.) Mama Guite calls for me to hurry up. The war is over. The French army has capitulated. (Marshal Pétain has taken charge in France. The winner at Verdun.) Mama Guite hugs me. The country aunt hugs me. Her husband is going to come back. (It gives me a funny feeling to have the war over.) Mama Guite says now we'll be able to go home. The country aunt tells her she has no need to hurry. (Marshal Pétain. The winner at Verdun. I mix Verdun up with Vercingetorix.) Mama Guite says she listened to Marshal Pétain on the radio at the neighbor's. He had a gloomy voice. (Neither Mama Guite nor the country aunt knows what a marshal is.) He said that the war had been lost, but honorably. (A chicken doing some cackling. A rooster some crowing.) And our prisoners? The defeat was so rapid that the Germans took thousands and thousands of prisoners. (Antoine is a prisoner. What's it like when you're a prisoner? Do they tie you up? When you play being a prisoner, the prisoner is tied to a tree. Do you remain a prisoner for a long time?) At the neighbor's there were a lot of people who don't have radios. They had listened to Marshal Pétain. They played the "Marseillaise." Everybody was stirred. (I don't know whether I would have been stirred if I had been there among them. How can that stir them, since the war is over? I'd like that, to sing the "Marseillaise" and to be stirred.) Mama Guite tells about it and you sense that it did something to her. She says that she thought about her father. He may perhaps have seen Marshal Pétain. (I sing the "Marseillaise," very low, to myself, but I am not stirred. What do you do when the war is over? What did you do while it was going on? Nothing, but we were having a war.)

—It was Pétain we should have had.

—They took good care not to put him in.

—They put in traitors like Weygand and Gamelin.

—Now that we have Pétain they're going to change their tune.

—Pétain, he knows how to handle the Boches.

—They can't have forgotten what he pulled off at Verdun.

—Pétain, he used to economize his men.

—He loved the common soldier.

—Lucky for us we still have him.

—Me, I trust Pétain with my eyes closed. I'm with him the whole way.

—And wherever it leads.

At the baker's they're saying that the war is over, that we have Pétain, that it's going to be another France.

At the grocer's they're saying that the war is over, that we have Pétain, that it's going to be another France.

At the hardware store they're saying that the war is over, that we have Pétain, that it's going to be another France.

At the shoemaker's they're saying that the war is over, that we have Pétain, that it's going to be another France.

At the dry goods store they're saying that the war is over, that we have Pétain, that it's going to be another France.

At the barber shop they're saying that the war is over, that we have Pétain, that it's going to be another France.

At the butcher's they're saying that the war is over, that we have Pétain, that it's going to be another France.

At the garage mechanic's they're saying that the war is over, that we have Pétain, that it's going to be another France.

They drink and they say by God yes vive Pétain.

We must give our heart to Marshal Pétain sing the

children from the independent school who march down the street two abreast.

Bystanders applaud them.

I applaud them.

People are proud of them.

I'd like to see what Marshal Pétain looks like.

I know he's an old man but I'd like to see his face.

I'd like to be going to the independent school and to sing for Marshal Pétain and to be applauded by people.

We're standing in rows. I am not digesting my breakfast café au lait. Everybody was to meet in front of the town hall. The men and women are in their Sunday best. The deputy mayor comes out of the town hall with a wreath of flowers. If I have to vomit I'll go behind a tree. They are saying good morning to each other. The mayor's wife arrives from home with a bouquet of flowers from her garden. She hands it to a little boy. A girl arrives with a bouquet. She has braids and a chain around her neck with a gold cross. The mayor says that we may now set forth. We set forth. It's churning in my stomach. We head down the main street. The houses are bathed in sunshine. The shopkeepers are in their doorways. They wave to us. They are gay. The mayor goes over and shakes hands with them. The little boy with the flowers is having trouble walking. All that is too heavy for him. The girl's thin dress is furrowing between her buttocks. I know I am about to throw up. We proceed around the square. The men are bantering. The women are gossiping. We go past where they do their bowling. From the open window of a house comes the smell of meat gravy. Acid's rising in my throat. It's bitter tasting. I swallow. We arrive in front of the monument to the dead. There are two men with bugles. One with a drum. The mayor motions to them. They play the "Marseillaise." It's out of tune. The bugles squeak. The men are at attention. Chins high. My stomach hurts. The mayor lays the wreath at the base of the monument. The girl lays her bouquet there. The little boy lays his too. He lays it crooked. There's some laughing. Some hand clapping. The mayor raises his arm. There is a roll of the drum. The mayor takes a piece of paper from his pocket. He takes his position in front of us. It's frequent that I do not digest café au lait. It's frequent that I have stomachache. The mayor says that victory or defeat is the law of war. That our soldiers did not break faith. That they are France's sons. That they had to cede before force. That we ought not to be ashamed of them. It seems to be going away. I wouldn't have liked to have had to vomit. Especially as around the monument there's nothing to hide behind. That we must trust in the future. That our France is eternal. That a military reverse shall perhaps serve to turn us into better Frenchmen. Our duty now is to follow Marshal Pétain. Marshal Pétain is a hero from the Great War. He is a wise man. To France he has made the gift of his person. Marshal Pétain shall guide us in the right direction. If yesterday's dead could rise up, as one man they would shout Vive le Maréchal Pétain Vive la France. Someone shouts Vive le Maréchal

Pétain Vive la France. Rolling of the drum. Everybody is pleased. The men are heading toward the café. The women are gossiping. I have the gripes.

They are tall. Broad shouldered. All the same size. In black uniforms. Strength, there it is.

They have boots. Black ones. Gleaming.

They are standing at the edge of the road next to their tanks. They're having something to eat.

Not all of them are blond, the way we were told.

They are tall. They are slender. They are lithe.

As we walk by we watch them eat. We came to see them. They pay no attention to us.

They are young.

They are sure of themselves. They have sober faces.

The ones wearing a cap have a death's head on it. A silver-colored death's head. They have silver-colored eagles on their chest. They have two little silver-colored lightnings on their lapels. Black and silver stands for death. The graveyard.

They are black and silver.

We make as if we were just walking past in front of them.

He has a dagger in his hand. A long shining blade. He cuts his bread with it. Above my nose he jiggles a piece of ham rind that he's pinching between two fingers. I smile at him. He does not smile. He tosses the rind into the grass down in the ditch. The others watched him do it. They are laughing. We don't understand. He takes the dagger by the tip of the blade and with a flick of his wrist plants it in the ground. Right next to the toe of his boot. The others have daggers. They plant them straight in the ground. With one flick of the wrist. They have eagles. They have lightnings. They have death's heads. They eat with their daggers. They are leaning back against their tanks. They are at peace. They are in France. They are at home. Tall. Broad shoulders. Black and silver. Strong.

—Pétain spared us from the worst. His name will go down in history.

There are green soldiers. They are less tall and less strong than the black soldiers. They have big helmets. They have rifles. They smile at people. They go into the grocery store. They buy packages of cookies. All the packages of cookies. They buy wine. Red wine. White wine. They buy aperitif. Byrrh. Cinzano. Pernod. La Suze. They buy canned food. All the cans of it. They buy cheese. They buy ham. Dry sausage. Pâté. When they leave, the grocer accompanies them to the door. He thanks them. He is wearing a cap. He gives them a military salute. The green soldiers chuckle. The green soldiers have their arms full of packages of food and bottles. The grocer watches them walk away. His wife restocks the shelves with packages of cookies. With canned goods. With liters of wine. With aperitifs. With sausages. Green soldiers enter the store. They buy packages of cookies. All the packages of cookies. The prices rise.

At the hotel-restaurant four of them came in together. Four green soldiers. They asked for an omelette. A seventy-two-egg omelette. Seventy-two eggs. An omelette, cheese, and champagne. For that the owner charged them triple the price. They paid. They left singing songs. Arms linked together. The owner of the hotel-restaurant said that the Boches aren't like what people had said. They eat. They drink. They pay. It's all as nice as nice can be. We don't mind having customers like that.

The grocer says the same thing.

At the bar the owner of the hotel-restaurant says it's the first time in his life he's made a seventy-two-egg omelette.

At the bar the grocer says that with these fellows around business is booming.

At the bar the wife of the owner of the hotel-restaurant says that this is the way things ought to have been since way back.

At the bar the grocer says that his wife said that the Germans she doesn't find anything wrong with them at all.

At the bar the owner of the hotel-restaurant says that well no in that regard there's nothing you can say.

The owner of the bar agrees.

At the grocery store the country aunt can't believe her eyes, the price of vegetables has doubled.

—It's that the prices aren't the same now that they're here.

—You can't pay them, all you have to do is go somewhere else.

—Things are beginning to be put back where they belong, you understand.

—This isn't Daladier or Reynaud anymore.

—Nowadays it's Pétain.

—Them at least, they aren't quibbling all the time over the merchandise.

—You seen their soldiers next to ours?

—And their equipment.

—We had horses, nags, they had tanks.

—We were still back there with hay and oats.

—And on top of that we were told they were barbarians.

—This war has had one thing in its favor at least, it's opened our eyes.

—They're first-rate people through and through.

—The officers are gentlemen, you can tell that just from looking at them.

—What they want is order and cleanliness.

—We're not against that, are we?

—On our side that's all we're asking for.

—We haven't been able to clean our house ourselves, so here they are doing it for us.

—If they're looking for a broom, that's my line.

—And those others, down there in Bordeaux, they're looking good, aren't they?

—They showed where their balls are.

—Behind their ears.

—In '40, we'd have had Pétain and it wouldn't have been the same jive.

—Might not even have been a war.

—Quite possible.

—Pétain has the Germans' respect.

—France is respected now.

The green soldiers are coming in to buy. All the rest of us squeeze into a corner so as not to be in their way. The grocer and his wife bustle about them. There's an officer. He has a silver cord attached to his dagger. He moves slowly around the store. When he points with his finger the soldier at his heels takes the product from the shelf. The grocer and his wife relieve the soldier. From there on they handle everything. Mama Guite says that where their hearts ought to be those people have a purse instead. We leave the store. Parked in front of the door of the grocery store is a military automobile with a soldier waiting at the wheel, and a motorcycle with a sidecar with two soldiers who are waiting too.

—That's always the way it is when there's an officer, the grocer says. Where it comes to organization they're the champions.

Mama Guite says we're leaving tomorrow.

The road is covered thick with refuse, broken objects, pieces of furniture, files of documents fluttering in the wind, bicycles without wheels, typewriters, dolls, new clothing, used clothing, torn clothing, strollers, shoes, a baby bottle, a bedside carpet, empty cartons, empty suitcases, empty crates, empty burlap sacks, a bolster, a man's shirt, tools, automobile tires, seats from automobiles, automobile headlights, a woman's wig, a rotting dead cat, you can see its ribs, its fur has been pared down, a dead horse, its eyes covered with blue flies, its pink-and-violet-colored tongue covered with blue flies, a metal bidet, mattresses, a man's hat, a pile of packets of seeds, gloves, a flattened wristwatch, a rabbit without its head, the road's a mess, strewn with lengths of wood and branches you've got to avoid with the car, Mama Guite drives carefully, she says she's not about to forget, she says in what state are we going to find the house, the road is greasy, sticky, black, blue, gray, with stains, little and big stains, dried blood you could say, Mama Guite says it's dried blood, the wooden barriers have been knocked apart, we drive over the pieces, that makes the cart jolt up and down, along the road there's nobody, the little towns are deserted, the houses' shutters and doors are shut, there are white road signs with black letters, written in German, Mama Guite says what are we going to find when we get there, we haven't passed one single car since we started out, there's a garage that's open, Mama Guite pulls up, the garage man says there's no more gas, Mama Guite tells him that if he doesn't want to sell gas he ought to be doing something else, the garage man tells her there isn't any more gas anywhere, there's no more gas in France and to drive around in a car you have to have a permit from the Germans, without a permit you're going to get yourself arrested by the Germans, and they don't fool around, at the wheel Mama Guite is scared, she says just so long as we don't meet any Germans, a rainstorm is flooding the road, it's difficult to see ahead, Mama Guite says that this way we aren't likely to run into any Germans, lightning flashes zigzag, inside the car the sound of the thunder is muffled, it's raining, it's making mist and big bubbles on the ground, it's raining, it's thundering, it's raining, at the end of the bridge we are ordered to stop by the German sentinel, a big green-gray rubber slicker reaching down to his feet, water's running off his helmet, his rifle's slung over his back, his face is dripping wet, Mama Guite shows him her open billfold, we have the right to pass, closing her billfold Mama Guite sees that instead of her papers she has shown the sentinel a picture of Saint Anthony of Padua, rain pours down, the city is dead.

Long and wide red streamers hanging all the way down the front of the grand hotel. In the middle, a white circle. Inside it, the swastika. Black. Everyone

104

stops to look. You aren't quite sure what it is.

(it's the swastika someone says)

(why on the hotel someone asks)

Word had got around that their tanks were due to come through town. To drive up the avenue. The sidewalks are thronged. There are a lot of old people. Children, women, and lots of old people. Nobody knows the time they're going to be coming through.

(there they are someone shouts)

(no that's not them someone says)

We've been there for at least an hour. There are more and more people.

(that the swastika someone asks)

(it's the Hitler cross someone says)

A big noise. A rumbling. The sidewalk shakes. The tanks. Their forward-pointed cannons protected by a gray canvas cover. Four abreast. They take up the whole avenue. Rank after rank of them. In tight formation. The whole thing advancing. It rattles the street.

(the Germans, all that out there sure tells you what you're dealing with someone says)

(and look at the spit-and-polish shape it's in someone says)

A black soldier is sitting on the front part of each tank. Another is standing in each turret. They are oblivious to us.

(shit ain't that something someone says)

(I wouldn't have wanted to miss this someone says)

The black soldiers sitting on the front hoods of the tanks do a back flip onto the pavement. They walk backward in front of the tanks. For ten yards. For fifteen. They halt. They stretch their arms out in front of them. The tanks advance. Advance straight at them. They place their hands on the hoods and spring aboard the tanks where they sit back down again. All of them at the same time.

(you see that someone says)

(you feel like you want to applaud them someone says)

The crowd applauds them.

(what the hell sort of a figure do we cut next to them someone says)

Some women throw bunches of flowers. The bouquets land on the tanks. The black soldiers don't even reach for them. The tanks roll over the bouquets. Some women are screaming. Some women scream Long live Hitler. They have bunches of flowers. They throw their bunches of flowers. The tanks keep straight on.

(yes but even so we oughtn't to be throwing flowers to them someone says)

(it's normal they're our conquerors someone says)

In the streets there is nothing but their cars, their motorcycles, their trucks.

They come out of the barracks in formation. Helmeted. Each carrying a submachine gun. A potato-masher grenade in their belt. They have little short boots on. They march in step. They are singing. A horse-drawn cart is going by. It bumps along over the cobblestones. Before them, perched on his seat, the driver raises his cap. On the sidewalk neatly dressed men raise their hats. A youngster gives a military salute.

In the trolleys the green soldiers offer their seats to elderly ladies and to pregnant women.

The elderly ladies and the pregnant women say thank you.

The elderly ladies and the pregnant women say you wouldn't get that sort of behavior from Frenchmen.

Marshal Pétain is old. He has a kepi with golden leaves around it. Under his kepi he has white hair. He has a white mustache. He has blue eyes. He has a complaining voice. Marshal Pétain is old.

Every morning in school there's the salute to the flag. We stand at attention.

We sing "Maréchal nous voilà."

Mama Guite has bought dozens of cans of food that we have been putting away in the cupboard that's in the little room. They told her that pretty soon canned goods may disappear.

—Soon you won't find any more canned goods, said the grocer Mama Guite knows.

Mama Guite says we'll never eat all these cans of things.

—You have a store of wine in your cellar? the grocer asks Mama Guite.

The grocer delivers cases of wine that we stack up in the cellar.

Mama Guite has coal delivered for the winter.

—This may be the last you'll be getting, says the coal man. Coal, with the Germans, it's going to be a chase to get your hands on any.

Mama Guite says that in order to sew she has to have it warm in her kitchen.

—If you like I'll put an extra truckload down there.

The coal man delivers another truckload of coal.

—With that you're fixed up for at least three winters says the coal man.

Mama Guite says she is crazy to have accumulated this mountain of coal.

We have a hen in a coop at the far end of the little garden. A black hen. She lays one egg a day.

I play dibs in the street with the guys. We play the knife game. You set the point on a fingertip, one fingertip after another, with the other index finger you make the knife somersault so that the point sticks in the ground. I'm very good at this game. I win lots of pennies. I save up my pennies in a blue cardboard box. I hide the box behind the cans of food in the cupboard. I sleep in the room that has the canned-food cupboard. Me and the guys, we imitate the air-raid siren. I'm the one who's best at imitating it. For my imitation I ask a couple of pennies. We imitate the muffled explosions of antiaircraft shells up in the sky. I'm the best at imitating them. I charge a couple of pennies for imitating them. Me and the guys, we snitch little cakes from the factory where they're made. They're called petits fours. Me and the guys, we eat them and we drink lemonades. Guttersnipes, that's what they call us, me and the guys. We say go stick it. We say my ass. Mama Guite gets complaints about me. Mama Guite tells me that I'll wind up on the gallows. That she's going to have me sent to a reform school. I pull an ear most of the way off a pupil at the Catholic school. Mama Guite whacks me with a broomstick and a poker. My arms are all bloody. Covered with bruises. Me and the guys, we'd like to get some eagles off German soldiers. Me and the guys, we sing "Maréchal on chie là." An old guy who has a beret down over the corner of one eye. He's from the ones in the Marshal's Legion. Medals stuck onto his lapel. They're skinny old guys with little mustaches like Hitler's. Who go around thinking they're hot shit. One old guy tells us we are dirty little Yids. I pull out my glider. The old guy has a whistle hanging round his neck. He toots. We take off. He toots. Me and the guys, we say that those old guys are old assholes.

The old assholes belong to the Civil Defense. They have their beret down over the corner of one eye. A shoulder bag. A gas mask. (In the gas mask you suffocate.) After dark they are in the streets and blow their whistle at lights in windows. You aren't supposed to see light in windows. They toot.

On almost every building there is a plaque next to the front door. It says in red shelter thirty persons.

On the landing of the top story in all the buildings there are bags of sand.

We poke a knife into the bags of sand.

We take out the sand and use it to play around with.

Mama Guite does not want to go down into the shelters.

She is afraid the building will collapse on top of her during the bombing.

But I go down there.

Just to see.

It's dark.

There's only one bulb for the whole cellar.

You see crowded together people rolled up in blankets.

People in pajamas.

People in bathrobes.

People who are shaking.

People who are crying.

People who are frightened.

People pretending they're reading books.

People explaining what the air raid's going to be like.

You see women nursing.

You see women getting themselves cuddled and kissed by men.

You smell sweat.

You smell piss.

You smell puke.

A man shot his dog dead with a revolver. His dog was afraid of the air-raid siren.

There's a blond who comes down to the shelter in a transparent nightgown.

The Marshal's portrait is on sale. Framed or unframed. You place the Marshal's portrait in the kitchen. In the bedroom above the bed. In the dining room. The Marshal's in the doctor's waiting room. The Marshal's at the post office. The butcher's got the Marshal. The baker's got the Marshal. The Marshal is in shopwindows. Several of my friends have the Marshal at home. Mama Guite says she isn't putting any of that in her house. They hand the portraits out for nothing. I've got one. I'm hiding it in the bottom part of the sideboard.

The wind cuts.
You have cards for bread. For meat. For fat. For everything.
The wind is icy.
You have a J3 card. You're entitled to four ounces of bread per day.
The wind is a piercing wind.
J3s are children and adolescents.
The wind rips you.
The bread I have isn't enough to get me through my day.
The wind claws.
Mama Guite gives me nearly all her bread.
The wind growls.
Not enough bread. Not enough meat. Not enough vegetables. Not enough milk. Not enough sugar. Not enough chocolate.

Not enough.

It's snowing.

The wind whistles. It's snowing. It's freezing. Mama Guite says fortunately we have fuel. Food you can do without in a pinch. You can't do without coal. It's cold. It's freezing. It's cold. Mama Guite makes hot soups. She gets potatoes from out in the country. You don't find any more anything. The shops become empty all of a sudden. You can't get anything even with the tickets. They haven't had their delivery. Tomorrow, maybe. There are lines outside the grocery stores, the meat shops, the butter-and-egg shops, shops where they sell food of whatever sort. It is cold. The wind bites. The line of people breaks up. They haven't had anything today. The shopkeepers pull down their shutters. One woman says there's pâté without tickets at a butcher's. Another says she was just there. They're out of pâté now. The shopkeeper says he was delivered only half of what he was sup-posed to receive. We go off to stand in line somewhere else. Without tickets you can have rutabagas. Swedish turnips. You have no butter for cooking them. No oil. No fat. The wind stings. It's cold.

In the grocery store, speaking in a low voice, the gro-cer Mama Guite knows tells her he can let her have some butter and cheese. Without tickets. A kilo of butter if she likes. At the higher price. In Mama Guite's opinion the grocer is overdoing it. In her opinion he has no right to charge such prices. Mama Guite says that she still asks the same price for her piece goods and her aprons. To have cloth and aprons you have to have textile points. With the textile card it's like with the other cards. You get almost nothing. You too you'll come around to the higher price the grocer says to her.

It's the black market.

The electricity is off for several hours during the day.

The gas is at its normal pressure only during meal-time hours.

Gadgets for sucking extra gas through the lines are manufactured by amateurs. They're sold on the black market.

Candles are no longer to be found.

To economize on coal we're buying peat. You get it on the black market.

To replace butter we buy beef suet which is like slime in your mouth.

They sell bundles of old newspapers. On the black market.

You crumple the paper into compact balls which you soak in water and afterward put into the stove you cook with or heat with.

The crumpled-up paper smolders slowly.

It gives out a bit of heat.

When evening comes your stomach has a knot in it.

Outside it's cold.

There's no more wool for knitting socks or gloves.

Wool does exist. On the black market.

In the house only the kitchen has heat in it.

You close the door.

You stop up chinks around the window frames.

When evening comes your stomach has a knot in it.

On the radio the Marshal says it serves us right.

He says that it is very handsome on the part of the Germans to leave us the little that they do.

Mama Guite has bought some butter, some cheese, and some ham. On the black market.

The bombers come at night. They are big planes. Lumbering and ponderous. Long before the warning sounds you hear the droning. It wakes you up. You are afraid each time. You are always on the alert. It wakes you up. You listen. You wait. It's a slow sort of noise. Maybe all they are doing is passing overhead in order to go on somewhere else to bomb. It's a steady kind of droning. Throbbing. Steady. Which grows little by little. Then grows rapidly. In the night. It's one in the morning. It's two. We get up. We get dressed. We put two blankets over our shoulders. Mama Guite has all her family papers and all her money in a little black bag, everything within reach. We listen. We wait. It's getting nearer. It's heavy. It's ponderous. It's frightening. You remain sitting on your bed. You are cold. You go into the kitchen. The stove still has a little heat in it. You heat some water for the herb tea. The water gets to a simmer. The siren cuts loose. It's for us. The sound is right overhead. We go into the little garden. We stand flattened up against the dividing wall. We are one against the other. You are cold inside. You look upward. You don't see anything. A little bit of moon. That heavy sound. The antiaircraft shells. Submerged, underwater detonations. Deep down. Hollow. I'm worried that there may be spiders in the wall where there are holes. I pull back a little. I shrink inside my blankets. The ground jumps. The sky explodes. Flashes in the darkness. We go back to the house. We are shaking. The airplanes are heading away. Less heavy. We heat the water back up. Without sugar the herb tea is bitter. We make ourselves a hot-water bottle. The siren goes off again. The nights when there are three alerts. The nights when you sleep. But do not rest. You think you are hearing something.

In the lines outside the shops some people are sitting on folding chairs.

The shopkeepers say that they have not received their delivery. They hold back merchandise in order to sell it on the black market.
The shopkeepers are becoming rich.
The shopkeepers are making fortunes.
We're hungry.
We're cold.
The shopkeepers sell everything. On the black market.
You can also trade.
Swap.
What's most sought after.
Tobacco.
Wine.

For a package of pipe tobacco you can have whatever you want.

Butter.

Meat.

Bread.

Or for a liter of wine.

Those who have nothing to trade and who have no money.

One of my pals faints in the street.

His mother goes through garbage cans after dark.

She brings home potato peelings and what's left of turnips.

My pal eats boiled peelings.

He says he is hungry and that it makes him cry.

BOF.

Beurre. Oeufs. Fromage.

Butter, eggs, cheese.

The bofs. That means grocers.

Dairymen.

Grocers who've got rich.

Dairymen who've got rich.

They're selling counterfeit bread cards. Real bread cards. Employees at the town hall who every month pass out the food cards sell them too. On the black market.

Those who are full-time black marketeers. They've quit their jobs, this is all they do now. They buy and sell. They trade.

The youngest go out into the country on Sunday pulling a little cart behind their bike. The farmers know them. They bring back butter, eggs, cheese, vegetables, and pork. They resell on the black market. They trade.

Antoine turns up one evening.

With a friend.

In this cold weather all they have is a jacket and a ragged pair of pants and a dirty shirt.

They have their hands in their pockets.

Antoine escaped with his friend.

They were captured in the Maginot Line.

Without having fought.

They didn't even know what was happening outside.

They had been playing pinochle from morning to night.

They had a sergeant major to climb their ass.

They say this shit war had been deliberate.

They say that this war is not a war against the Germans but against the Russians.

Antoine is a Communist.

So is his friend.

They didn't want to fight this war either one of them but once you're in a war it might as well be for some purpose.

The cases of artillery shells were filled with empty champagne bottles.

In the arsenals who filled these cases?

Who had orders to fill them?

Ammunition cases like those.

The officers would say don't worry your head about it.

The officers were all right wing.

It isn't the Germans they're afraid of but the Soviets.

It isn't fascism they're afraid of it's communism.

(Antoine explains fascism nazism and communism to me. Italy, that's Fascist. Germany, that's Nazi. The USSR, that's Communist.)

Before being cornered like rats the men dealt with the officers.

A few of them got a bullet in the head.

The smarter ones had taken off before the arrival of the Doryphores.

(Antoine explains to me that you say Doryphores for the Germans because doryphores are little insects who eat the leaves of potato plants and reproduce quick as a wink.)

The proof is that not all that many officers had been captured.

Antoine says that he and the others had been taken for goddamned fools.

From beginning to end.

That the Germans they had been taken prisoner by had treated them like sheep.

Now he said we're going to have to show them that we've got balls.

It's not over with yet.

Whatever you see going around in green or black pump a shot into its belly.

We're going to show them that us guys don't belong to the right.

We're going to show them that we know who we went to war against.

Not against the USSR.

Not against the Land of Lenin.

(Antoine explains to me that Lenin's real name was Ulyanov.)

Against Hitler and the whole European right.

The Ribbentrop-Molotov Pact is a political maneuver by Stalin in order to gain time and manufacture weapons.

(Antoine explains to me that Stalin is the Little Father of Nations.)

The Soviet army is a great army.

It is together with it that we must fight against the Nazis and against all the fascisms in France and elsewhere.

We didn't undertake '36 for nothing.

(Antoine explains to me that '36 was the strike to better the lot of the working class.)

They think they put us in their pocket.

That started with the war in Spain.

(Antoine explains to me that the war in Spain was already the Communists against the Fascists. The Communists had lost. The winner had been Franco. Franco is a general.)

They're making a big mistake.

They've got themselves into one hell of a battle.

The guys from the Communist cells are going to regroup everywhere.

Doryphores and Fascists, they're in for a rough time.

The first thing though has got to be to liquidate Pétain.

A swine, that's what Pétain is.

Him and his band.

They're the France of the two hundred families.

(Antoine explains to me that the two hundred families it's the families of big manufacturers who control the money and manipulate the government to get hold of still more they never have enough of it.)

You talk Pétain you're talking Cagoule.

(Antoine explains to me that Cagoule is a Fascist secret society that acts through terrorism. A secret society that was trying to come to power and that is in power today with Pétain.)

Pétain was a leader of the Cagoule.

The Cagoule is French fascism.

Hatred of the worker.

Money.

The government.

The Cagoule is French capitalism.

(Antoine explains to me that capitalism is the exploitation of man by man.)

Antoine is ravenously hungry.

His buddy too.

They haven't eaten in three days.

We lost the war, we lost the war.

Now it's the Occupation, the Occupation.

The Boches have taken what is rightfully ours, the Boches are in our house.

We ought to have defended ourselves that's all.

The Occupation nobody gives a damn about it.

Nobody gives a damn about the Boches.

Nobody gives a damn about anything.

Eats are all that counts.

Eating. Eating. Eating.

Buying stuff to eat.

Having stuff to eat.

Making stuff to eat.

Eggs.

Chicken.

Leg of lamb.

Into the stew pot. Into the oven. Into the frying pan.

With lots of butter.

Filling your belly.

Stuffing yourself to the gills.

Drinking a couple of good glasses.

Having a cigarette.

Eating. Drinking. Smoking.

Eating. Drinking. Smoking.

Eating. Drinking. Smoking.

Life it's what happens at the table.

The Occupation and all their other fuckups it's not our business.

Let them work it out together.

Blum, Daladier, Reynaud, Pétain, the Boches, they're alike enough to be the same thing.

Now it's the Americans who're beating up on us every night.

Those assholes unload at ten thousand feet.

From an altitude of ten thousand feet the bombs you drop fall wherever they have a fucking mind to.

The target isn't touched one time out of two.

There are people killed.

The Yanks what do they care if they wreck our whole country.

If they like us so much they can just send us some of their chow and the rest of the crap they've got.

Where they live it's the land of big eats.

They get their three squares every day over there.

They have a full plate in front of them.

If we had a full plate we wouldn't ask for anything else.

Problem of the Boches we'd look into that later.

If those assholes weren't taking everything we have there'd be no reason why we couldn't hit it off with them.

Collaboration is first of all seeing to it that there's beefsteak for everyone.

The Seligmanns went around and sold things at markets and fairs. They have disappeared. Their car was left parked in front of their house. They didn't tell anyone they were going anywhere. There has been no further sign of them. Everyone knows the Seligmanns are Jews. At the market they were liked. Very obliging people. Some are saying they may have been arrested. Why? For doing what? Being Jewish is enough.

The Germans are arresting the Jews. Why we don't know. Because they're Jews. That makes several weeks that no more has been seen of the Seligmanns.

—You hey what's your real name?

—It's the one I'm called by.

—We know you're not French.

—I am too.

—You've got a Spaghetti first name.

—So does he have a Spaghetti first name.

—You're Jewish and you say you're Spaghetti.

Mama Guite is making smocks for the baker's wife. Every other day once night comes I go to get a big round loaf of white bread without tickets at the bakery. You mustn't let anyone see you. It's black market. The bread we get is good and puffed up. Crusty. Good and white. To make it the baker sifts his flour. The flour they deliver to him is gray. He says that there are all sorts of things in it. Beans. Chickpeas. That it's shameful to see flour like that. He sifts it. Every second evening we have white bread.

Mama Guite is entitled to tobacco with her card. She doesn't smoke. She trades her tobacco for butter.

You're entitled to wine. We trade it for sugar.

I resell to neighborhood people the fancy cookies that are stolen out of the factory.

At the factory they must have noticed something. They've put in bars over all the windows.

They're talking about this General de Gaulle. A general who is in London. A felonious general. (A felonious general is a general who is a traitor to his country.) He spoke on the radio. Nobody heard him. In the neighborhood nobody heard him. They say here's another one who wants to catch the public's eye. Still another one who wants to get himself talked about. He ought to have done some fighting when it was the moment for that. They say they're fed up with the military. We already have Pétain for us that's enough. The English if they'd wanted they could have come over here and got their asses shot off. They're such great allies of ours that they are bombing us. De Gaulle that name sounds like a joke.

The bofs are raking it in.

I'll be doing whatever needs doing in the warehouse. (It's a big immensely long shed with wooden shelving going high up on the walls, the shelves are loaded with woven materials, blankets, canvas for awnings and covers, sheets, handkerchiefs, packets of socks, skeins of raffia, rope, string, women's stockings, loaded with bolts of woolens, with packages whose paper wrapping has yellowed with time and of whose contents no one has any idea, loaded with tons of textile merchandise, and with, at the far end of this shed, a tiny windowed office.) I'll be storekeeper. I will make bicycle deliveries. There is a large two-wheeled metal cart that attaches by a curved rod underneath the bicycle seat. Even empty, the cart is heavy. I'll sweep up in the warehouse and in the courtyard every Saturday. It's a big courtyard. With a tree. A plane tree. At the end of the courtyard, the warehouse. Opposite it, the house where the watchman lives. It's he who locks up the entrance gate at the end of the day. It's he who opens up in the morning. I'll have a key to the warehouse. I'll be the first one arriving there in the morning. I'll often be the last one to leave. I am responsible for the key. A big iron key. There are millions and millions in merchandise in the warehouse. I will come to know the customers. The middlemen. The reps. I'll keep some of the accounts if I show I'm capable. I'll answer the telephone when the boss isn't there. If I can manage all that I'll have a good salary. (The good salary is barely enough to feed myself on.) If I am not able to handle it they'll take on a secretary. (If they take on a secretary my salary will be reduced. They do take on a secretary, because the boss sleeps with the secretary up on the second floor, in the afternoon. On the second floor there's mattresses and still more cloth, and more blankets, and more pillows, and more gloves, and more brassieres, and more Turkish towels, and more dishcloths, and more everything you can imagine. My salary will be reduced.)

I am working at the warehouse.

I measure cloth. The lengths of ordered cloth that I have to deliver to customers.

In the afternoon I make up skeins of raffia and pack them into sacks. That burns your hands.

In the afternoon I wind paper string into balls. That burns your hands.

I make packages. Enormous packages the carrier comes to pick up every morning. I band them with strapping. The strapping is on a spool. It's a thin strip of flexible iron. That cuts your fingers. I have bandages on all my fingers.

I help the carrier load his truck. He yells at me. He says I don't move fast enough. He says I'm a crybaby.

I load up my cart. That makes a small hill of stuff that I secure with string.

I do the deliveries.

Certain customers give me a tip.

I begin in the morning at six forty-five.

I go to work on foot. I figured that the price of streetcar tickets mounts up to too much by the end of the month.

I economize.

I leave home at six-fifteen.

It's dark. Cold. There are streets where the wind goes right through you.

I take along a piece of bread that I eat while walking.

I go past a big yellow-and-gray building with flaking-off stucco. In front of the entrance are two German soldiers. They stamp their feet. They talk in German. On their chest they have a big half-moon-shaped sign hanging from a thick chain. There are letters on the sign. That must be heavy around your neck. They wear long green coats. Belt and shoulder straps over them. Grenade at the side. I walk by in front of them. They pay no attention to me.

I arrive when the watchman opens the gate.

The watchman wears a beret cocked over his eye. Like the old assholes from the Legion. He has a little mustache. Like Hitler.

He doesn't say hello to me. I don't say hello to him.

I open the warehouse.

I break some sticks for kindling.

I go and get a bucket of coal from the back of the warehouse.

I light the stove.

I get down to work.

One morning, in the street, there's a dead man lying there. It's the first dead person I have seen in the street. A man curled up on the pavement. His hat has rolled to the edge of the sidewalk. He has blood under his nose. He has blood on his forehead. He has blood on his shirt. I make a detour around him. I go a distance and stop. I look back at him. A man comes along on a bicycle. He says to me get out of here kid don't look at that that isn't for you to look at. The bicycle's lamp projects a thin blade of light. Headlights have to be painted over in blue or black. You leave nothing but a horizontal sliver in the middle. There's a hollow feeling in my stomach. I take a few steps. I look back. The shape on the ground is dark. I wonder whether the man is really dead. Maybe the man isn't dead. If the man isn't dead what should you do. I run off out of fear.

On the radio there's Charles Trenet and Maurice Chevalier.

Lines in front of shops.

Lines in front of all the shops.

Policemen saluting the German officers.

Towing my now empty cart I stop outside movie houses. I look at the photographs tacked up in the entrance. I know the names of the film stars. Annabella. Mireille Balin. Jean Gabin. Eric von Stroheim. Fernandel. Victor Francen. Louis Jouvet. Raimu. Jules Berry. Viviane Romance. Arletty.

The girls have tight skirts which stop at the knee.

The girls have on summer dresses that the wind lifts up when they are riding bicycles. You see their underpants. Blue ones. Pink. White. Black. I follow them with my bike and my cart. They know I do.

The warehouse secretary has a tight skirt. When she bends over you see her underpants. She paints her legs so that it looks like she has stockings. Silk stockings cost a lot on the black market. All the girls paint their legs. They draw a brown line along the calf and on up the thigh for the seam of the stocking. The warehouse secretary sits in the office with her thighs a little apart.

The men are prisoners.
You can die tomorrow in an air raid. You want to make the most of life while you've got it. The women long for men.

On streets that mount the load becomes too heavy, I get off my bike, I haul my cart on foot straining over the handlebars, the street rises, it's heavy, the weather is hot, I'm sweating, it hurts in my legs, I'm out of breath.

The boss says to me little asshole, little snotface, little good-for-nothing, little shit-for-brains, little bastard, he says I'm bound for hanging.
Yet I have worked hard.
He says to me I'm docking you on your pay.

An officer wearing a long coat with red lapels gets out of a military automobile in front of a big hotel. A soldier holds the door of the car for him. At attention, other soldiers salute him. With his black boots below the coat, this long green coat, those red lapels, you'd say he was some prince. You'd say it was like in the movies.
I stopped in order to look. There are more than one hundred kilos that I have to drag in my cart.

The German women-soldiers, we call them the gray mice. In the street they are always with an officer.

They're saying that if the Germans had freed their French prisoners the whole country would have collaborated with the occupant. That France and Germany are made to get along together. Just release our men, that's all it would take.

The wives of the prisoners send food packages to their husbands. You've got to find that food. Buy it. On the black market. You need money.

Everybody is after money.

You can have a girl for a pound of butter.
A bar of chocolate.
A kilo of sugar.
A pack of cigarettes.
A pair of stockings.

You can have a girl for nothing.
They have short skirts.
They squat down.
They cross their legs.
They make themselves up.
They buy makeup. On the black market.

The women have shoes with wooden soles.

On the radio there's Suzy Solidor.

The Marshal says that France is paying the price of a painful experience but that her ordeal will ennoble her. The Marshal gives France a new motto. *Travail. Famille. Patrie.* The Marshal wants there to be a return to the soil. Let everyone become a peasant again. France is a land of peasants. The French must remain peasants.

You can obtain the Francisque for free to put in your buttonhole.
If you are for Pétain you put the Francisque in your buttonhole.

They say we are in the Nono Zone. In the Non-occupied Zone. The Germans are everywhere however.

Everyone is going to see *The Jew Süss* at the movies. It's a German film.

Coming out after seeing *The Jew Süss,* some young people are yelling down with the Jews.

Policemen are shaking hands with those who had yelled down with the Jews in front of the movies.

At the movies everyone is going to see *The Well-Digger's Daughter.* It's a French film.

Coming out from *The Well-Digger's Daughter* some young people are yelling Vive Pétain Vive la France.

Coffee is being replaced by roasted barley. They're buying roasted barley. On the black market.

Huddled against the airhole at the base of a building. A dark blue suit. Shoeless feet. White socks. His hands are tied behind his back. The cord has entered into the flesh. Deep into it. It is violet colored. Swollen around the cord. His eyes are half-open. Glassy. His hair is stuck by blood to his temple and cheek. His mouth is open. Dark blood on his chin. An expression of awful suffering. The passersby cast an uncomfortable glance his way. The passersby act as if there isn't a dead man on the sidewalk. An ambulance arrives. They say that the stiff over there? The stretcher. The ambulance drives off. There is an almost round black stain where his head was.

I remain for quite a while in the street sitting on my bicycle. I think about suicide. What it must feel like when the bullet enters your head. Or your heart. I see myself bringing the barrel of the pistol close to my temple. To my heart. Or putting it into my mouth. I have the feeling that in the mouth it must blow the skull open.

I am in a corner of the warehouse. The salesman has not seen me. He walks over to a shelf. He opens his briefcase. He stuffs two packets of socks inside. He shuts his briefcase again. He whistles to himself. He slips his briefcase under his arm. He calls is there anyone here. I do not answer. He steals two more packets of socks. He goes away.

The curfew starts at ten o'clock at night.

A young woman is walking down the street.
A black Citroën slows to a halt beside her.
Two men wearing brown leather coats and dark hats spring out of the black Citroën.
One man immobilizes the young woman with one arm, puts his free hand over her mouth.
The young woman struggles.
She is thrown into the black Citroën.
The doors slam shut.

The black Citroën drives off.
The passersby pass by.

A young man is walking down the street.
A black Citroën slows to a halt beside him.
Two men wearing brown leather coats and dark hats spring out of the black Citroën.
One man immobilizes the young man with one arm, puts his free hand over his mouth.
The young man struggles.
He is thrown into the black Citroën.
The doors slam shut.
The black Citroën drives off.
The passersby pass by.

The men in brown leather coats and dark hats are the Gestapo.

The Gestapo they say.
No one dares to ask what the Gestapo is.

The Gestapo is arresting Jews.

The Jews that's the Jews.
That's special.

Marching in ranks down the street the German soldiers sing "Lili Marlene."

I am working on the second floor the secretary finds some reason for coming upstairs she pretends she's looking for something she doesn't have anything to do up here I am arranging the shelves the bolts of material are heavy to lift she asks if she can help me I answer that I don't need anybody she laughs shaking all her hair she sits down on a pile of sacks she lies back with her arms propping her up she is in a tight-fitting summer dress with little flowers her body is thrust forward her slender body her dress meanders up high onto her thighs she smiles at me without taking her eyes off me her little breasts leave a hollow of supple cloth between them she sticks the tip of her tongue out between her lips she spreads her thighs a little she spreads them a little the underpants are white it's deep and dark between the thighs and the underpants are white I don't dare to look at her any longer I go about my work I know that I have on undershorts that have a hole in front I turn around her with my bundles she is beside me in back of me in front of me she tells me to switch off a lamp I do what she tells me to do she arches her feet all that's touching the floor are the ends of her big toes with her heels she slides off her shoes real leather shoes of dark blue leather they cost a small fortune on the black market she is barefoot her toenails are red it's the first time I have ever seen red toenails I think about the blood in the street she says let your work be you little silly you are how old thirteen fourteen I say thirteen and a half that makes her laugh her laugh comes from deep down in her throat from deep down in her belly she raises her legs all of a sudden all of a sudden she spreads her thighs her dress is in a turmoil around her underpants she says get it out come here and take me I'll suck you afterward when you've got my taste on you the air-raid siren goes off she says we don't care come here take me get it out I want to see it.

Some women are saying all of them are prisoners there's nothing left anywhere to get yourself a screwing from.

The boss says to me you're going to recopy this into the account book. I recopy some figures written on a dirty scrap of paper.

The boss says to me if someone asks me who keeps the firm's books I've got to answer that it's me.

The boss says to me that if I say what he's telling me to say at the end of the month I'll have a little bonus.

I am proud to be keeping the books.

Tarp-covered trucks. Convoys of tarp-covered trucks. Motorcycles with sidecars. Helmeted soldiers. Soldiers on foot. Soldiers in the streets. Soldiers on guard at doorways. Soldiers walking about. Motorcycles with sidecars. Tarp-covered trucks. Convoys of tarp-covered trucks.

Nighttime alerts.

I remain in bed.

The next day we hear that a section of the city has been hit by bombs.

Last night it was the airfield.

They missed it.

Bombs on the houses all around.

On the radio there's Philippe Henriot. He speaks every night.

Heading the administration there's Pierre Laval.

They say Laval has made a lifetime out of switching allegiances.

They say Laval is a traitor.

They say Laval is collecting millions from mineral water.

They say Laval has the looks of someone you'd never trust.

They say Laval is the king of collaborators.

They say Laval wants to sell France out to the Boches.

They say Pétain is senile.

Laval wears a white tie.

It's early in the morning.

It's springtime.

A spring morning.

Two or three women on the sidewalk across the street.

Who are watching.

I pull up on my bicycle.

At the ground-floor window there's a big woman in tears who's shrieking.

A little girl next to her.

She's shrieking I am Jewish.

She's shrieking they want to arrest us because we're Jews.

The big guy with the hat is pulling her backward.

She is hanging on to the stiles of the window with both hands.

The big guy with the hat and the coat.

He tears the big woman away from the window.

The little girl is crying.

The big guy with the hat is closing the shutters.

Our eyes meet.

Lock.

Gimlet green eyes.

I do not lower mine.

He lowers his.

I believe he is ashamed.

He closes the shutters.

I'm afraid he's about to come out of the house and arrest me too.

I get onto my bike.

All day long I keep seeing that big woman who is shrieking.

It's the STO. Which is the Service du Travail Obligatoire. The French have to go to Germany to work. Germany is short-handed. The Reich's soldiers are defending us against the Soviet Beast. The Russian Bear. The monster Stalin. The Communist bastards. The Jew bastards. Communism that's the Jews. The Soviet Union that's the Jews. The Jews are aiming at worldwide hegemony. Seeking to dominate the world. To run the world.

To have all the world's money. The brave German soldiers are dying for us on the Russian front. In defense of Aryan Europe. The French must participate in the European effort by going to work in German factories.

The bofs get richer.

The Marshal says that we have to bring about the National Revolution.

Philippe Henriot says that we have to bring about the National Revolution.

Doriot says that we have to bring about the National Revolution.

Déat says that we have to bring about the National Revolution.

Philippe Henriot says that we must rid ourselves of the Jews.

Doriot says that France is jewified.

Déat says that the Jewish problem must be resolved.

The Marshal says nothing about the Jews.

The Marshal has met with the Reichskanzelier. Chancellor Hitler. They shook hands.

The Gestapo is arresting Jews.

The French police are arresting Jews.

The boss says to me little asshole if you are asked anything about the warehouse you keep your little mouth shut or you'll find yourself booted out of here before you fucking know it. What goes on here is nobody's business. If you are able to handle yourself right later on you'll become a representative of the firm. In the meantime do your job.

I know all the customers.

The customers slip me a coin or two so that I'll tell them whether we are expecting the arrival of any merchandise in the course of the week.

Any kind of merchandise at all.

Everybody is interested in buying everything.

At whatever price.

Buying. Selling.

I've got them all straight.

Monsieur Meyer whom I like.

Monsieur Blank whom I like.

They say to me you keep us posted on arrivals we will be nice to you.

When I deliver to their house they give me a tip.

Madame Sachetti whom I like.

Madame Médicis whom I like.

There are those who steal in the warehouse believing I'm not there believing nobody's around.

There are the secretaries who steal stockings pull them on right away and get rid of the empty packaging upstairs.

There is one secretary I saw open the safe in the office and quickly shut it when she saw I was looking at her.

The safe is never locked.

The safe is full of money.

When the secretary is fired because the boss is tired of going to bed with her and I am the only employee left in the office I too open the safe I look inside I touch the bills.

Millions in cash.

I could buy myself all kinds of stuff on the black market.

They have painted big yellow stars on the windows of the shops.

They have written Yids in yellow.

People stop. Look. Chuckle.

—No one knew that it was a Yid store.

—They are all Yid stores.

—Not all.

—Nearly.

They have stuck posters on the windows of the shops. Jewish shops.

People stop. Read. Chuckle.

—Still another Yid.

—It's a good thing they've arrived here. There'd be more Yids if it wasn't for them.

—That's the reason why we have to give Pétain a helping hand.

They painted yellow stars.

They wrote Yids.

They broke the shopwindows.

They threw mannequins out onto the sidewalk.

They painted yellow stars on the sidewalks in front of the shops.

They tried to burn them down.

Yellow stars.

Smashed-in windows.

Sidewalks with yellow stars.

—That was the Yids' stuff, they're taking what they want.

They are taking away the mannequins.

It frightens me.

Charles Trenet he's the Singin' Fool.

He sings "Y'a d'la joie."

The bofs are getting richer.

The Gestapo is arresting the Jews.

All around me there is nothing but stealing, lying, compromising, lust for money, selfishness, indifference, corruption, hypocrisy, disguised prostitution, violence, cowardice, baseness, self-seeking obsequiousness.

I am thirteen years old. Fourteen years old. Fifteen years old.

I am learning about mankind.

Mankind is mainly shit.

They are all part of the black market.

The others are hungry.

The boss is leaving on a trip. He stacks up the money from the safe. He wraps it in a big package which he puts on a shelf between some bolts of cotton. I am sweeping the warehouse. He tells me proudly that there's ten million in there. He rubs his hands together. That's a habit he has. He leaves me a list of everything I must do while he is away. There isn't any secretary. He tells me they're sluts. You have to put them in bed and after that send them home. With the prisoners business all their cunts are on fire. They can't do without it. You beginning to make out where it comes to women? Little fucker. Just let me catch you I'll cut it off you there and then. He says bah! Wartime's got its good side. If you know the tricks wartime's a happy hunting ground. War is for the ones who are smart. Go for your share you little fucker. If you're thinking to put a little extra into your pocket now's the time. Just tell them that deliveries are charged for. So much per kilometer. Same as elbow grease isn't put in for free neither is knee grease. On the black market it costs as much as any other grease.

I now charge for my deliveries.

My pal asks me if I have any money.
A little.
How do I earn it?
Working.
Do I earn a lot?
No.
Do I get myself any extras on the side?
Yes.

I am a Yid son of a bitch but he likes me all the same.

My pal wears the Francisque on his lapel. He puts up posters for National Revolution. For La Rassemblement de la Jeunesse. For Déat. For the Marshal. He is making money. They have it to spend. It costs them plenty. There's money and cunts. At section headquarters there's fun all the time. They screw the cunts on the tables. Soon maybe he is going to have a gun. In there all the guys have guns. It's up to some Germans in civilian clothes. The Fritz they're not what you'd call outgoing. When they are it's stick straight to business. They're running the show. They're the ones who pass out the moola. The leader is a very funny guy. It's the Germans who got him out of prison. He had been into a bit of this and that. With women. Hustled a little if you like. In there there're several hustlers. That's how come there are cunts. And not shy I might as well tell you. There's one who's the queen of cocksucking. What they don't like is the Communists and the Yids. They say they make black pudding out of them. Watch out with your Yid looks bubba. My pal is a short fat guy without any sort of color. He wants only two things in life. To have money and to have a good time with cunts.

I make a delivery to a shop.
The shop is empty.
I call.
No answer.
I wait.
I call.

I turn around. I am looking toward a dark corner.

At the end of an arm sticking out between two mattresses there hangs a white hand.

My blood freezes in my veins.

I leave.

I pedal as fast as I am able to with the weight in my fully loaded cart.

A new secretary says to me we take the money that's in the safe and we take off the two of us. You won't be sorry I have a special jigger in my pussy. The boss is a dirty old bastard. It'll teach him. You and me we've got a right to live too. He fucks every day. Why not us. With what's stashed in there we can make a great life for ourselves. If he wants to give us trouble we can report him for black market activity to Economic Supervision. In the filing cabinets there's everything. She's looked through them. Order vouchers. Falsified invoices. With that we're covered. We'll go to Collioure. She went there when she was little. If I want we can rip one off right now so I can see what she's able to do in bed. I shut the door of the safe. She spits in my face.

France has no more army. France is beaten. France is occupied. Germany puts a rebirth within our reach. We must seize this chance we are offered. This chance is called Collaboration. Germany and ourselves, we have a common enemy. Communism. The communism that seeks to destroy all the values for which our fathers and grandfathers fought and sometimes paid with their lives.

The values of the true France and of the true Europe. We are a Catholic people. France is the eldest daughter of the Church. Our two great nations shall form an empire. The Germans are neither our friends nor our enemies. They are our brothers.

The Marshal speaks in his sexless voice.
Henriot speaks in his nasal voice.
Doriot speaks in his barking voice.
Déat speaks in his bureaucrat's voice.

To replace the period of military service the Marshal and Laval come up with the Youth Camps.

Twenty-year-old Boy Scouts.

Former noncommissioned officers in the French army are schooling young men in Fascist discipline and the Fascist ideal.

Many wives of prisoners have taken jobs.

Many women who have never worked are working now.

Many women who have never smoked are smoking now. (On the black market the price of tobacco and its value have suddenly shot up.)

Many wives of prisoners are raising their child alone. (The child its father did not know before being called up.)

Many wives of prisoners have a lover.

Many women are finding out that they can live alone.

Surrounded by passersby two policemen with flat caps and wearing capes (the pigs on wheels, because they are always on a bicycle) slap a young man, giving him a bloody nose. The air is cool.

Toward dusk, in an empty street, quite a distance ahead of me I see a body sprawled on the street, I am frightened, I am sure that it's a dead person who'll have blood all over his head, on his chest, that there will be blood on the pavement, my heart is pounding, I slow down, my cart is loaded to the maximum, I've taken shortcuts to minimize my effort, if I turn and go the other way that will add a quarter of an hour to the trip, I walk my bike, I advance cautiously, I grit my teeth, I know I am going to be looking at someone dead from a wound which has bled, I draw closer, it's a big piece of wrapping paper, I had been so afraid, I climb back on my bike, I am crying.

If you have a good radio set you can listen to London. It's jammed but you are able to hear. On Radio London it's de Gaulle, it's the resisters who talk. The Resistance, it's for throwing out the Boches.

The boss goes into partnership with another boss.
Batteries have become scarce.
They are going to set up a factory to make batteries.
I'll be working in the warehouse and in the factory.

I steal some books. At night I read. I do not understand all the words.

What do they do with the Jews they arrest?

Nobody asks himself what they do with the Jews they arrest.

Nobody's asking himself about anything.

What they want is eats.

Drinks to drink.

What they want is money.

Money is what war is about.

Those who don't have any money can just as well shut their mouth, no one's going to listen to them.

Because they're such stupid assholes.

If they aren't even capable of black marketeering it's because they're assholes and too stupid.

The Jews? What're they?

No one gives a shit about the Jews.

They filled their pockets with it.

Now they're being made to cough it up.

Let them take care of themselves.

Nobody likes anybody.

Wartime, that's how it is.

At the warehouse we've stopped getting visits from Monsieur Meyer.

In the street people act as usual. You see German soldiers. You pass them in the street. In the trolleys there are German soldiers. At the post office there are German soldiers. On the terraces outside big cafés there are German officers. German officers with Frenchwomen.

Whores is what women say. Go to bed with a Boche, never. You have your man imprisoned in Germany and you'd go and sleep with those bastards. They'd really have to be whores. What are they thinking of. The men say yes. Ah yes.

The ones who are just keeping body and soul together. Those who are having trouble making out at all. Who aren't making out at all. Who haven't anything to sell. Who buy a little on the black market. Who haven't enough money to buy more. Who say Pétain or some other. Who say Laval or some other. Who say if we could just get enough not to be hungry. Who say if we could just give our kids food like before. Who say the pudgy pink-cheeked ones are eating every day in the black market restaurants. Who say that in there you have all you want of whatever you want. Who say you need only plunk down the price at the exit. They serve the meat hidden underneath the vegetables. Who say there have always been the sons of bitches and the others. Who say this isn't going to lead them to happiness. Who say after the war there will be scores to settle. Who say it without believing it too much. Who just say it. Whatever.

In the bars there are the days with and the days without.

The days with you can have yourself an aperitif.

The days without you can have yourself an ersatz aperitif.

The days without the owner of the bar or his wife is in the back room serving those who can pay black market.

They arrest him because he was denounced. The French police arrest upon denunciation. The Gestapo arrests upon denunciation. The French are denouncing one another.

I empty the office ashtrays. I put the cigarette butts in a can. In two weeks' time I have enough to make a packet of tobacco that I wrap up in some newspaper and sell to one of the salesmen or to a customer. With this tobacco I can also get butter, oil, sugar, chocolate, bread tickets.

As concerns the priests, the bishops, the cardinals, all is going well. It must be going well as concerns the pope. The priests distribute blessings. The bishops distribute blessings. The cardinals distribute blessings. The pope distributes blessings. Everything receives blessings. The starving. The cops. Fascism. Nazism. The wounded. The dead. The victims. The black market. Pétain. Laval. The Others. The Kommandantur. Paris. Vichy. The prisoners. The STO. The women. The elderly. The children. The murderers. The informers. Big business. Collaboration. The return to the soil. All is good. All is well. In their robes they are untouchable. In their charges. In their archdioceses. In the palace at Rome. The curés are fat. The pope is thin. Their hyp-ocrites' looks. Their profiteers' looks. Their looks of through-and-through phonies. Their parvenu looks. Their pleasure-lover looks.

The Gestapo is arresting Jews.

Everybody's told to report to their town hall.
I don't go.

My pal says I'm giving you a rod because I like you.
I hide the rod in a sack that I put underneath my dirty
underwear.

I despise, I hate, I despise that old idiot's voice of his
which seems to be coming out of his cap with its oak
leaves. I despise, I hate, I despise that simpleminded old
man. The Winner at Verdun comes across as an old asshole. Clean and tricked out. At the big hotel in Vichy he
eats carrots. We're told that he is abstemious, a frugal
eater. An example for the country. The country eats fru-
gally because it hasn't any food. Pétain is a frugal eater
because he can no longer eat. A trembling old man. A
wily old man. An ambitious old man. He incarnates. An
old bourgeois. He incarnates narrow-minded France.
Holy-water France. The France that's had it up the ass.
He incarnates everything that France is not.

The boss returns from his trip. I see him hunting
between the boxes and the rolls of cloth for his millions.
I know that if I wanted to I could keep still and become
a millionaire. I don't dare. I find his stash for him. He's
in ecstasy. I say to myself that at least he's going to give
me a thousand-franc note. He sticks his money back in
the safe. And get to work little asshole what the hell did
you do while I wasn't around. By Jesus I'll show you if
I'm going to pay you for jerking off. The next time I'm
pinching his money. With all the dough this bastard's

got he's still sending me to his house to put the ashes in his stove through a sieve to see if there are any pieces of coal I can salvage. While I'm gulping down coal dust his four-year-old kid is playing on the rug with five-thousand-franc bills. I'd sure like to take one from him but I'm worried what if the bills have been counted.

The black Citroën stops in front of the door to the building. The driver and the three others. With the hats and the leather coats. Faces like hatchets. White faces. No eyes underneath the brim of the hat. Hard fast-moving shadows. One hat remains by the door. Gun in his pocket. Hand gripping it. Not tall. Not heavy. Closed up. There's noise on the stairs. He pays no attention. To that or to anything. The driver starts the motor. The hat opens the car door. An old man is being pushed forward. Yanked. Shoved. He is tottering. They have hold of him by the hair. At the back of his head. They have one of his arms twisted behind his back. He is in pajamas. Blue-striped ones. Barefoot. They push him into the black Citroën. Its doors close. It drives off. On the other side of the street there's a line outside the butcher's. It's the day for pâté without tickets.

To get anything you have to be signed up with the shopkeepers.

We're entitled to some dried bananas. There aren't any. Not this week. We're entitled to some raw sugar. There isn't any. Not this week.

My pal likes Pierre Blanchar.

Pierre Blanchar is a movie star who rolls his eyes and raps out his words.

He also likes Harry Baur.

My pal's got money.

He doesn't have anything to do during the day.

He goes to the movies.

With some cunts.

My pal likes Maurice Chevalier.

Maurice Chevalier is a singer who has a straw hat on his head and who does the Parisian accent.

My pal says he wouldn't mind being in the movies.

My pal would like to sleep with a cunt from the movies.

Suzy Prim.

She's a blond. With a big mouth. Sleepy eyes.

My pal wants his cunt out there in the field. By the time the war ends he'll be set up for life.

One or two cunts in the field.

With his friends he walks into cafés. At the cash register they say Gestapo. They want the money.

With those who refuse they come back at night. They smash the windows.

The next day they come across.

My pal really gets a kick out of that.

The machines have arrived. Big agglomerate machines. The agglomerate is compressed powder that you place in brass tubes. The machine forces a graphite pencil into the middle of the agglomerate. Over the end of the pencil the machine forces a little copper cap. In a four-and-a-half-volt battery there are three agglomerates. You connect the three pencils by soldering a thin lead wire to connect the three copper caps. For the contact. It's minute work. You scorch your fingertips with the soldering iron. If you complain the foreman says you dumb cunt if it's me. If it's a girl bitch you don't yell when you're sucking. The foreman is a slave driver. I solder. I burn my fingers. I lug around the cases of batteries. They weigh tons. I bust my butt. The foreman yells. He is constantly yelling. Lazy bastard you want me to spread your cheeks. I'm going to give it to you it'll get you to move. I want to kill him. I'm bringing my rod one of these days and I'm blowing him to hell. Whenever he gets the urge he says to the girls you drag your ass over here I've got a cock that's seized up you're going to oil it for me. They go off to the toilets. The girl returns and sits down. She is ashamed in front of the others. Those who don't want my cock they can get the fuck out of here.

A mass for the prisoners.
A mass for the fighting men.
A mass for the war widows.
A mass for France.
No mass for the Jews.

They have a broad navy-blue beret that slants down over the temple.
The insignia looks sort of like a paper clip.
They have a jacket and trousers that are navy blue.

A dark blue shirt and a black tie.

A machine pistol at the hip.

They are social failures without trade or profession.

Some are idealistic young men misled by the propaganda put out by the Marshal, by Laval, by Darnand.

Some are pimps.

Alcoholics.

Former jailbirds.

Cretins.

Hoodlums.

Habitual criminals.

Onetime policemen.

That's the Milice.

The Milice do the work of the Gestapo.

The Milice escort the Gestapo's men during arrests.

The Milice search houses.

The Milice break down the doors of apartments in the middle of the night.

The Milice rape women.

The Milice torture.

The Milice do whatever they like.

The Milice are French.

The Milice arrest Jews.

The heads of the Milice are Frenchmen.

My pal is in the Milice.

—There's two or three of us when we go to work.

We ring the bell. We start kicking on the door. When they open we shove the door into their faces. We say Milice. Just take it easy. We search the cunts. We mess the place up. We locate the money. In tin cans. In drawers. In kitchen cupboards. In the gas stove. We say what sort of money is this. Where does it come from. Black market. Confiscated. They're shitting green. We take the money into custody. We take charge of the jewelry. Soft job being a Milice. Everybody keeps out of our way. Even the Fritz they respect us. We're the Marshal's army. We're putting the house in order here in France. The bofs' money is ours for the taking. If I need a little loot I go after it even in civilian clothes. Just my rod. I say Milice. I smash everything in the house. I put the cash in my pocket. Talk about fun. A cunt if she's all alone I put it to her. I stick the rod under her nose and she spreads. Yids we bring home about ten of them every day. They're passed around by the guys who give them a little workout. You say Milice to them and they shake like leaves. The Milice are a great bunch. Darnand, yeah quite a guy. He came around. We got to see him. He said that we're the France of tomorrow.

The French right.
French capitalism.
French bourgeoisie.
French clergy.
French police.
French Milice.
French shopkeepers.
Your average Frenchman.

The factories are cranking it out. The money is rolling in. Order prevails. The system's doing all right.

In honor of the Marshal families are giving their son the name Philippe.

An inspector from Economic Supervision is often a former inspector of police.

You have him take a seat in the office.

He asks for the bookkeeping.

Into the cash book you insert a large-denomination bill.

He pockets it.

He checks the figures.

He says that everything looks fine.

I'll be coming back.

He comes back each month.

Philippe Henriot is on the air every night. Every night all of France listens to him. Everything he says sounds like it's true.

—You listen to Henriot last night?

—Doesn't even amount to a half-ass that guy.

Our batteries are called Light of Day Batteries.

I work with the mixing of the acids. The black powder. The powder for the agglomerates.

The black powder is churned for several hours in a wooden mixer that I operate by turning a crank.

Inside the nook where I work it's one thick cloud of acid fumes.

The particles in the air glow in the light from the overhead bulb.

The stuff burns your mouth your nose your throat.

The stuff permeates your clothing.

For protection you're entitled to a leather apron.

The powder eats the leather apron.

Working with me I had this little guy.

His apron eaten through in front.

He would cry.

He said it hurt him there.

He meant his balls.

He showed me.

Burnt. All red.

I went and got hold of the foreman.

He said his balls I'll eat them for him.

I went and spoke to the bosses.

The bosses wanted to have a look.

The little guy showed them his balls.

The bosses threw him out of the factory.

I'm in the acid cage from seven in the morning till six at night.

It causes the skin to peel off your ears.

We are entitled to two electric batteries per month.

The foreman doesn't give them to us.

The women workers ask to have them.

He says two batteries for a suck off.

I ask.

He says I'm going to hook one up to your ass and I don't mean one of the four and a half volts it'll make you sing.

He has his personal supply.

I steal batteries from him.

He says the first son of a bitch I catch with his hands on my stuff I'll flatten him.

I peddle the batteries in the tobacco shops.

The boss takes me to eat in a big black market restaurant. He has an appointment there with a supplier. I have a notebook. I am supposed to note down what the boss tells me. It's a big place. White curtains everywhere. Round tables. White tablecloths. Three glasses in front of each plate. Knives and forks made of silver. It's warm. It's white. A headwaiter escorts you to your table. As they enter German officers give the Nazi salute. Arm outstretched. They take off their caps. They take off their belts with the pistol and the dagger. They hang all that up on the coatrack. They smooth their hair with the palms of their hands. They sit up straight. Stiff. Satisfied. They are like they were invited. The owner knows almost all of them. They shake hands. The officers speak French. They join the owner at his table for a digestive. They are smoking cigars. Some have eaten grilled lobster. Some have eaten leg of lamb with thin string beans. Salad has been eaten. Cheese has been eaten. Several kinds of cheese. Ice cream has been eaten. With whipped cream on it. The supplier says words in German to the officers. I have eaten too much. Driving back to the warehouse in the car the boss says to me well little asshole you saw how I wrapped them around my little finger, didn't you. The Boches for me they're a pushover. Actually they're pretty likable. It's them we've got to do business with from now on.

I knew him by sight. A skinny guy. A big nose. Red. He had sort of a leaning toward the bottle. A guzzler you could say. Worked on a lathe. His wife and two kids. In two rooms. When he'd come back after having one too many he'd spend the night on the stairs. Still in overalls. The black Citroëns. Three or four of them. Four. Milice everywhere. The door smashed in. The wife who's crying. The kids. They beat the guy up in his own house. They drag him out of there bleeding. He's singing the "Marseillaise." One of the Milice hits him in the back of the head. He falls down onto his knees. Blood trickling from his nose. From his mouth. From his eyes. From his ears. They load him into a black Citroën like he was a package. There are spatters of blood on the sidewalk. It's a Communist someone says.

We aren't seeing Monsieur Blank at the warehouse anymore.

You hear shouts in the street at night. You hear running. You hear shots. You look out through the closed windows. There is no light in the streets. You see nothing. You hear shouting. Running. You hear shots.

At the movies it's Jules Berry and Arletty.

You have a shirt, you sell a shirt. You have a pair of shoes, you sell a pair of shoes. You have some handkerchiefs, you sell some handkerchiefs. You have a watch, you sell a watch. You have a cushion, you sell a cushion. You have what you have, you sell what you have. You sell in the streets. In the cafés. In the trolley cars. You propose what you have to sell. You sell it at once. To someone who keeps it or to someone who in his turn sells it for more a little later. With the profit you buy something else which you then sell. Money. Money. Money.

Pierre Laval is saying that we have to make an effort. A further effort. The Germans are making efforts on our behalf. We've got to make some on theirs.

The Marshal is traveling around France. There are crowds gathered to see him. To cheer him. To sing the "Marseillaise" when he comes out onto the balcony.

Vive Pétain! Vive Pétain! Vive Pétain! Vive Pétain!

Inside the massed crowd a worker fails to remove his cap. A police sergeant smacks him on the head with his kepi. The worker removes his cap.

Vive Pétain! Vive Pétain! Vive Pétain! Vive Pétain!

It's the Republic that led us to tragedy. Our misfortune is owing to the politicians. The French State is going to efface this stain.

Vive Pétain! Vive Pétain! Vive Pétain! Vive Pétain!

France is a land where traditional values are going to be restored to their former place.

Vive Pétain! Vive Pétain! Vive Pétain! Vive Pétain!

On the balcony beside the Marshal are some French policemen, some Milice officers, some dignitaries, there's the bishop, there's the cardinal, they greet the crowd by waving their plump and dimpled hands.

Vive Pétain! Vive Pétain! Vive Pétain! Vive Pétain!

We saw Pétain. Fine figure of a man. At his age. Straight as a ramrod. You sense that this is a man who loves France. With all his heart. A soldier. A great soldier. Flowers are thrown in his direction. The little ones were given a view of him. They were lifted up onto shoulders. There were women in tears. Some men too. They shouted Vive Pétain so much their throats were sore. The finest day in our lives. One cannot understand why the English don't come to terms with a man like this. Could well be though that they're coming to terms in private. That is without anyone knowing. You know what people are saying. People are saying that de Gaulle is Pétain's nephew. De Gaulle and Pétain it's the same. What they want is to get us out of the hole. For that the first thing is for there to be no more Jews. When there aren't any more Jews getting in between us everything will work smoothly. The Boches will leave. They won't have anything more to do in our country. The Marshal promised that they were going to free some prisoners. That would really be fine. Their poor wives who're waiting for them. Not all of those wives have waited for them. There are a lot of streetwalkers too. Well anyhow. The main thing is that some return. Pétain gives you confidence. You saw how he took the little girl up in his arms to kiss her. Like a kindly grandfather. He must certainly be a grandpa. You can tell. You can see he is a good man. Back in '14 he was like that already. The men loved him oh yes they did. In '14 Pétain was their god. As long as we've got him we're at least not in the shit. He's a man who can talk to Hitler if need be. We're glad to have seen him.

Police and Milice. They salute each other in the street. They shake hands. They talk together. They are friends.

There is a cordon of Milice around the one that was shot down.

They have laid his machine pistol and his beret on his chest.

There is a long rivulet of blood on the sidewalk.

The Milice are out of their minds.

Murderous faces.

The slightest thing and they could start shooting.

I pedal past with my cart.

Last night there were two alerts.

I tell my pal who's in the Milice that I have a pal who is so hungry that in order to walk in the street he has to lean up against the walls. He says he'll let him have some counterfeit tickets. He gives me a big punch on the shoulder. Hey Jew-boy don't let them get at your kidneys.

There is a cabinet officer for prisoners' affairs. He goes to Germany to inspect to see if our prisoners are being well treated. Monsieur Scapini, that's his name. He is blind.

Hitler made a trip to Paris. He arrived early in the morning. Empty Paris.

A trolley car full of German air force pilots on leave is attacked by Resistance people. Revolvers. Submachine guns. Grenades. All that stopped the trolley. There it stood. Machine-gunned. We go to look at it. Metal sides ripped up. Windows all blown out. Pieces of glass as far as the opposite sidewalk. On the other side of the street. Traces of blood. Some gray forage caps and a pair of eyeglasses. Thirty dead and thirty wounded they said. Others said fifty dead. They said there weren't enough ambulances. Two soldiers are guarding the trolley. The driver has been killed. They know it's the Resistance.

Explosions.
At night.
Bursts from automatic weapons.
Cries.
Next day blood on the ground.
Official buildings wrecked.
Windows torn away.

Explosions.
At night.
Cafés blown up.
The collaborators' hangouts, their cafés.
Maybe. You don't know.
A crater.
Rubble.
Bits of window glass.
Window glass reduced to dust.

They are seizing hostages. Anybody at all. At random. The Resistance's actions are driving them nuts.

On the radio Philippe Henriot says that our German friends are showing a great deal of patience with us who in killing defenseless German soldiers in the street are disregarding even the code of honor that prevails in war.

A Milice is killed in the street. They seize ten hostages in the street.

The Milice torture.

In Germany there are camps for the Jews.
They arrest the Jews.
They take the Jews somewhere where they are crammed together.
They beat the Jews.
The Milice torture the Jews.
The Gestapo tortures the Jews.
They load them into cattle cars.
They carry the Jews away.
They put the Jews in concentration camps.
Nobody has any notion of what a concentration camp is.

The French police know that there are concentration camps for Jews in Germany.
The prefects of the French police know that there are concentration camps for Jews in Germany.
The Milice know that there are concentration camps for Jews in Germany.

The Marshal knows that there are concentration camps for Jews in Germany.

Pierre Laval, Philippe Henriot, Jacques Doriot, Joseph Darnand, Marcel Déat know that there are concentration camps for Jews in Germany.

It isn't known what they actually do in order to torture.

The Milice.

The Gestapo.

It is thought that they rough people up.

On a winter afternoon three men who come running down the street three men who have on coats lumberjacks berets pulled down tight on their heads each one has a knapsack on his back a knapsack in front over his stomach and the knapsacks are preventing them from running fast each has a grenade in his hand they look like they were very poor they are running they turn at the street corner a little later there's this explosion.

The tall redheaded young woman had been arrested in the street. She was a resister.

—The resisters they're hoodlums say the old Legion of Honor assholes.

—If that's how it is we're heading for a civil war says a gentleman.

—The resisters they're Communists says a woman with a shopping basket.

—They're asking who are they these Resistance people?

—They say it's de Gaulle.

—The London one?

—That's right. The London one.

—The Resistance it's the Yids say the old Legion of Honor assholes.

My pal in the Milice asks me if I listen to Radio London.

I don't own a radio.

My pal in the Milice tells me that if I hear someone who's listening to Radio London I've got to tell him.

Those who listen to Radio London are traitors.

Those who listen to Radio London they arrest them and they give their balls a rubdown.

Those who listen to Radio London they're all resisters.

The Resistance it's the Yids and their jewified friends.

Darnand has said so.

I go to people's houses and I listen to Radio London.

It's some thumps on the bass drum.

It's London speaking the French speak to the French.

It gives the news the true news.

It sings Radio Paris lies Radio Paris lies Radio Paris is German.

There are coded messages.

Personal messages.

You can't understand them. They start you laughing. You stop listening.

You can't hear well. It's jammed by the Germans.

I say to my pal in the Milice Radio London boy they don't sound very impressed by you guys.

He says to me all those Yids they won't stop their yapping until we've turned them into hash.

My pal in the Milice has changed from the way he was before.

My pal in the Milice doesn't act like he's my buddy anymore.

One day he says to me I don't know you I have never known you I don't know whether you aren't a traitor.

Now and then I catch sight of him in the street with others in the Milice.

He doesn't look at me anymore.

It's the Battle of Stalingrad.

—Looks like Fritz has started getting it in the ass somebody says.

Riding in the trolley my boss says to some German soldiers who don't understand French:

—So what's the word, man? Nippy weather in Stalingrad?

The boss is buying by the truckload. The boss is selling by the truckload. He says you've got to speed it up with your moneymaking. This won't stay up as long as the Tower of Pisa. The Tower of Pisa is the tower that leans. I can't see what that has to do with it. The bundles of thousand-franc bills pile up inside the safe. I take some to the bank. In a briefcase. Two or three days later the safe has filled up to where it was before.

One day while showing me the safe overflowing with bundles of big-denomination bills the boss says to me all right what would you do with all that money if I gave it to you? I think about it. Then he says well what would you do with it? I say I don't know. He says you see you're nothing but a stupid little shithead not even worth a kick in the ass. I give you all that moola and you don't even know what to do with it. You're all alike. What you like is being flat down and out. Money and you don't go together. You'll never have any. Money you've got to like it in order for it to like you. You're all just a bunch of stupid jerks a bunch of fucking down-and-out dwarfs. Piles of money like that you're not going to see them often in your life. So take a good look at them and lick your chops. That money there isn't for the likes of you. He rubs his hands together. He's feeling good. I'm tempted to tell him that I wouldn't mind sticking a match in there under that money of his.

They put on the anti-Bolshevik exhibit. The anti-Jews exhibit. Everybody wants to see it. There's a crowd waiting outside. You stand in line to get in. Milice at the entrance are frisking everybody. In the rooms inside there are Milice everywhere. Carrying machine pistols. They are keeping close watch. It's an exhibit of big photographs and of written things. Photographs of former cabinet members. Jews. Photographs of movie actors and actresses. Jews. Photographs of writers. Jews. Photographs of musicians. Jews. Lenin. The Russian revolutionaries. Jews.

—Get a load of the schnozz on that one there people are saying to each other and laughing.

—Tells you it's a Yid.

—Lousy-looking bunch the people are saying and they grin at each other.

—Lousy-looking Yids.

There is an old man with some white beard showing on his face. He is stock-still. As if weighted down. Our eyes meet. His face is sorrowful. As he moves past he lays his hand on my head. He goes away. The people haven't stopped laughing.

The shopkeepers have put up signs in big letters in their windows. This is a French store.

The boss's partner, who is the father-in-law of the foreman in the factory, goes into the nooks and crannies of the warehouse with a long pair of scissors in his hand. With the tips of the scissors he gives the bigger spiderwebs a tap. The spider darts forward. He snips off its legs.

Laval and the Marshal have invented the Relève du STO.

Volunteers are to go to Germany to replace the workers who have been sent there.

For each volunteer one forced laborer will be set free.

There aren't any volunteers.

The Marshal talks about the Relève on the radio.

Laval talks about the Relève on the radio.

The Marshal talks about the Relève in the newsreels.

Laval talks about the Relève in the newsreels.

There aren't any volunteers.

There's no further talk about the Relève.

Outside the building where the Milice are located you can hear screams that reach all the way into the street.

At the entrance there is a Milice with his machine gun.

The Milice torture.

At the end of the bridge, at six-thirty in the morning, there are dead bodies piled up on the sidewalk.

The first time I am frightened by the sight.

I take off.

The next day I stay and look.

There are four bodies in the pile.

You don't see the faces. The faces are turned away toward the wall.

There is a pulled-up pants leg. The leg is blue.

The hands are tied behind the back.

There is a thin mist. A haze. Damp. Gray.

On the pile of dead men are three hats and one cap.

The next day there are other dead bodies.

The day after that there are other dead bodies.

The day after that I know they're there.

There are some which are floating in the green river.

Arms stretched out ahead.

Facedown in the water.

Being slowly carried along by the green water.

The LVF that's the Légion des Volontaires Français.

Volunteers to go and fight in the German army on the Russian front.

Guys without a job.

Guys just out of jail.

Bachelors.

Lost souls.

Same thing as with the Milice.

With a German uniform on with the helmet and the little shield painted on the helmet all that gives them confidence again.

That gives them some importance again.

Darnand tells them that they are going to smash the Communist Beast.

That thanks to them Europe is going to be purified.

That for this purifying France will be indebted to them.

Darnand tells them that they are invincible.

Skimpy little man. The uniform brings his spirits up. The rifle brings his spirits up. The LVF brings his spirits up. People look at him now. He struts. He is the New France. He is the Europe of Tomorrow. He can be threatening. He can be dangerous. Underneath, he doesn't amount to anything. He is afraid. He is amazed to be in the LVF. Amazed he is wearing the uniform of the conqueror. That he impresses those around him. He knows that he is despised even so.

The steady drumbeat kind of sound.

Deep heavy sound.

Sledgehammer sound.

Nighttime tracer bullets.

Tracer fire rising in the nighttime sky.

Sizzling green lines.

Explosions.

Far off.

Nearer.

To the left.

More to the right.

Antiaircraft gunfire.

The sky lights up.

Fairy lights which descend slowly out of the sky.

The softly glowing sky.

Explosions.

Great showers of red flashes.

Illuminated globes of cloud.

Windows flapping in the blast from explosions.

The panes falling out of them.

Children are crying.

Crazed mothers with children are crying.

Elderly people with canes.

You see the airplanes in the sky.

Black cutouts.

American bombers.

Heavy bombers.

A din without letup.

It rubs your nerves raw.

Tightness in your chest.

Shrilling of whistles in the street.

In the shelters.

Those who are listening.

Those who are reciting Hail Marys.

Those who are pissing in their clothing.

Those who cannot bear being underground any longer.

Those who come rushing up the stairs like lunatics.

A gas mask forgotten in the corner.

The square and the streets have been plowed by the bombs. Wails. Groans from within the rubble of collapsed shelters. There are survivors. A torn-off arm up in a tree. A split-open head in the gutter. Dead people. A woman sitting on the ground. Out of her mind. Dead children. A severed arm in the debris. A foot. A hand. A trunk. The Red Cross. Active women. Useful. Effective. Blankets. Warm liquids. The men are at a loss, helpless. Dead bodies. Bleeding men. Bleeding women. A corpse cut wide open. Tears. No cries. Tears. They're digging. Earth. Pebbles. Mutilated bodies. An arm underneath the shovel. A dead arm. The weather is superb. Clear and warm.

Coffins lined up in broad daylight.

Hundreds of coffins.

The cardinal giving his blessings.

In the street two police inspectors, one on each side of me, grab me by the arms. They have tight hold of me. It hurts from their grip. We cross through the courtyard. One inspector says junior just keep your trap shut.

It's happened so fast I haven't yet understood. We enter the warehouse. They push the door to behind us. I start to tell the boss that they stopped me in the street. The inspector tells me to shut up. They let go of me. I remain standing there. They ask for the boss's identity. The boss shows them his papers. They ask what I do in the warehouse. I start to answer. Shut up they tell me. The boss says what I do. The inspector says you get your hands up. Don't act cute. I raise my hands. I hear the sound of someone running. The boss is upstairs. The inspector is running after him with his pistol out. The boss tries to climb up through the skylight onto the roof. The inspector wraps him up around the legs. They come back down. Pistol stuck in the boss's back. The inspector says we're taking these two fuckers in. The kid too the inspector asks. The two of them the inspector says. Call a wagon. The inspector gets on the telephone. There aren't any more wagons. Shit says the inspector. Put the cuffs on them we'll take a trolley. Me and the boss they attach us together with the handcuffs. The inspectors have us between them. They have hold of us by the arm. We head for the trolley stop. The people don't dare to really look. We step up onto the platform of the trolley. It's crowded. Approaching a stop the boss gives me a signal with his eyes. He wants me to jump off with him. We jump off. The momentum of the trolley throws us off balance. We collide with each other. They get hold of us again. The inspector says it's going to be the whole show. These two sons of bitches you saw them says the inspector. You're in for a workout says the inspector. The station is gray inside. Dirty. Stinking. A young woman is sitting down her face is being slapped and she's crying. One of her cheeks is swollen. Her lips are open. Her lips are bleeding. A young man is standing up against a gray wall. It has dirt on it. They are kneeing him in the groin. Typewriters are clacking. Nonstop slapping. An inspector belches. The boss receives a slap. I put my arm up in front of my face. They unfasten us. They attach us to pipes running along the wall. I am thirsty. The boss has been bleeding from the nose. He does not look at me. Time passes. The inspector says let the kid loose. The inspector takes the handcuff off my wrist. The inspector tells me now scram and don't let me see you in here again giving us trouble. The boss is attached to the pipe. Outside it's night. The street feels cold.

I don't know why they arrested us. I ask. The boss says learn to keep a hold on your tongue. I'm in a rented room. You'll bring me my meal at noon and in the evening. I've got to keep indoors. You'll be careful. You look to see if there's anyone following you. If there's anyone who looks suspicious you head off for somewhere else. You come back later. If anyone asks you any questions you don't know anything. For the food you go by my wife's place. She'll give you what's needed. If she asks you where I am you don't tell her anything. The only ones who'll know are my partner and you. You'll get extra for your deliveries. The big thing is to keep your mouth shut.

It's a tumbledown little building. Real poor. With poor people in it. Poor people and workers. Women who yell. Yelling kids. Women doing the wash out in the courtyard. The stairway is narrow. Dark. The wall has crusts. He's on the top floor. I knock quietly on the door. I say boss it's me. The boss opens. I pass the basket in to him. I don't know why the boss is in hiding.

In the evening next to the hospital there is a man selling meat wrapped up in newspaper. Black market meat. He's holding a plaited shopping basket. Inside the basket is the piece of meat.

—He works at the morgue someone says.

The English air raids are low altitude. The bombs hit their targets. There are fewer people killed. Sometimes none at all.

The warehouse is closed.

I see the boss's partner going in there with his scissors.

Often he comes back out with boxes of women's lingerie.

When the curtain has been drawn in the factory office you know what it means.

There's a big secretary who's continually laughing.

For the workers it's in the toilets.

The toilets are at the far end of the courtyard.

The foreman is on the lookout.

He fines the guy and the girl who come out of the toilets.

He says got your allowance eh you fucker?

Slut he says to the girl you owe me a suck.

That's her fine.

The girl snickers.

The foreman says won't be long before I've been done by every one of these cocksucking sluts.

We're heading toward some more hiring.

The lilacs are out.

A sunny afternoon. You hear the crackle of rapid-fire weapons. It's farther up. I go to see. There are some helmeted SS. Machine guns leveled. Some Milice. Some inspectors. Some police officers. The Milice are marching along the street in front of the SS. They are advancing in a line. They position themselves in a semicircle. One knee on the ground. Some SS officers are conferring. I watch them from a distance. The sun is hot. There's firing. There are blasts. From grenades. A little square building. Its green shutters are closed. Grenades. It's on fire. Black smoke rising straight up. In puffs. The Milice advance toward the house. The SS stay where they are. Three of them there to the rear. Three and two officers. Through one of the hospital gates come an old man and a young man and a girl. It's strange to see them suddenly come out of the gate in the wall around the hospital while everybody is watching the little house that's burning. The SS officer points with his hand. An

SS grabs the old man by the arm. He pushes him up against the wall. Gets the young man. Pushes him up against the wall. The girl. Pushes her up against the wall. One short burst. Another. Another. Rivulets of red blood are running down the hospital wall. I move away. I hold back from running. An inspector beckons me over. He says you know anybody around here? I say I live three streets away. He points to the three bodies. He says you want to make the fourth? I say no. He says kid you've got about two seconds to get your goddamned ass out of here. Walking away from him I feel sure he is going to shoot me in the back. I follow the wall as it turns the corner. I think I am going to faint. I don't want to run. I keep from running. Grenades.

The RAF keeps bombing.
From having heard it so often you end up knowing that it's the Royal Air Force.
The English planes.

There are attacks every night.
The radio says terrorist attacks.
It's the Resistance.

They say the resisters that means being in the *maquis*.
The *maquis* you don't know where it is.

On all the walls they put up wanted posters for the terrorists with their pictures.

Trains are being blown up.

We know that the Germans are no longer safe from danger.

We know that the Germans no longer have the edge.

They are taking hostages.

—Though they know for a fact where they're headed now they're still not done giving us a bad time a man says.

—The country's waiting for de Gaulle that's what's happening a man says.

Tied to the pier of a bridge, a tricolored cross of Lorraine inside the tricolored V for Victory flies above the waters of the river.

People are leaning over the parapet to see.

Access to the bridge is now forbidden to pedestrians.

Firemen in a rowboat come and take down the cross of Lorraine.

They're done for a man says.

The Milice are out in groups of three or four, stalking up and down the streets, scowling at everyone. They say you Gaullist bastard to this person or to that one. They call for identity papers. At gunpoint. A cigarette drooping from their mouth. They deliberately lower the shoulder on people going by. The people make way. Avoid looking at them. Quicken their steps. The Milice have grins on their faces. They call out insults. There are some who are drunk. They are stopping automobiles. They are making the driver and the passengers get out. They examine their papers. They search the automobile. One man receives a slap. He starts to protest. He is bashed on the head. You stinking Gaullist the Milice say. If people look to see what's going on they say if anyone doesn't like it just let him open his fucking mouth. Stinking Gaullists that's what we wipe our asses on. They make filthy remarks to women they encounter on the sidewalks.

At a street corner in front of a bar are the corpses of three members of the Resistance in the positions they were finished off in. Which was three days ago. A Milice stands guard. The corpses have placards on them. You're afraid to come close enough to read what they say.

Two Milice machine-gun a man to death in front of a movie house.

Two Milice kill a young woman outside a café.

During the night a bomb went off in front of the Milice's local headquarters.

The woman laughs. The machine gun chatters. The woman falls. The blood is flowing from her cheek. The sparrows peck upon the sidewalk.

It's early. The foreman comes into the warehouse.

He says find yourself work to do that isn't in here. I go out into the courtyard. In the courtyard the plane tree is green all over. I pick up an interesting-looking pebble. An officers' car drives up. A convertible with two officers in it and the driver in front. The foreman bows and scrapes to them. The gate is closed again. In the factory the boss's partner says to me what are you doing screwing around in here. I go back out into the courtyard. The driver of the car looks at me. I walk over toward the street. In his cabin the watchman is looking too. A girl on a bike. Bare thighs. I don't see her underpants. I hear the motor of the car. It drives past in front of me. The two officers sitting in the back. I return to the warehouse. It is locked shut. The foreman isn't in the warehouse or in the factory either. I go to where I do the soldering. I get going on some work. It is midday. It's when you go to eat. I have some bread and some chocolate. I stand around in the street. The column of tarp-covered trucks arrives. A column of eight trucks. They park in the courtyard. The warehouse doors are wide open. The soldiers load up the trucks. One after the other. Without stopping. Eight big trucks. The watchman asks me what's going on. Since he's never said a word to me before I don't answer him now. The trucks set off. The foreman shuts up the warehouse. The empty warehouse. I go to where the boss's wife lives to get the midday meal for her husband. On the landing outside his room I say boss it's me. I tell him that the warehouse has been emptied by the Germans. He goes white. His face is sunken. White. He says come on quick take me there on your bike. We arrive at the warehouse. The warehouse is locked. In the factory office there's a ruckus. The boss and the partner. They're fighting. The boss has a cut lip and a bloody nose. He's so angry he can hardly see. The bastard he says to me he's sold everything to the Boches. I have nothing left.

The Boches are working the black market says the boss.

Along the whole length of a street a wall is covered with tricolored posters with the cross of Lorraine in the center.

—De Gaulle is going to arrive and he and Pétain are going to reach an understanding people are saying.

You hear talk of the FFI and of the FTP.
Forces Françaises de l'Intérieur. Francs-Tireurs et Partisans.
The FTP they're the Communists.

It is evening and a drunk and unbuttoned Milice is yelling in the middle of the street.
—Bring your Gaullists right over here! I'll make them piss!

German automobiles everywhere in the city.
German trucks everywhere in the city.
Motorcycles.
Sidecars.
At night tanks move through the streets.

All night long.

—They're hauling ass says one man.

The four blockhouses with horizontal loopholes at the four corners of the prefecture are empty.
Without soldiers.
In one blockhouse there is a tabby cat that goes in and out.

They are removing everything from their offices.
They are removing everything from their requisitioned hotels.
Trucks filled with crates.
Trucks filled with cartons.
They are in a hurry.

Bombs go off every night.

You see some German soldiers that are Chinese looking.
Slant eyed.
Mongols they're called.
No one knows where they came from.
They're saying that they're not to be trusted.
It's said they're raping women.

All the soldiers you are seeing in the streets now are old.
There are also some aged fifteen. In patched-up uniforms. In uniforms a couple of sizes too large. Bunched

in at the waist. In helmets that are too big. With packs that are too heavy. They don't look as if they know where they are. They are pasty faced.

It's said they have cleared out of the barracks.
The sentries they've left are just for the sake of appearance.
Old guys.

—They don't have anything left to eat says one man.

The bay horse is close to dying in front of a neighborhood movie theater.
Its big belly is giving jumps.
It lifts its head a little.
It lets out a rattling sound.
Its head falls back down.
It strikes upon the pavement.
The horse waves its four feet.
Beneath its tail watery dung and blood are flowing.
In spurts.
Regularly.
Like each time the horse breathes.
It has big dark eyes.
Its big black eyes are crying.
Real tears.
Lips pulled back from over the yellow teeth.
It's breathing hard.
It's in the act of dying.
The haberdasher's shop on the square was serving as a mailbox for the Resistance.

The haberdasher on the square was given away.
The haberdasher on the square is dead.

The Milice arrest Monsieur and Madame Franji who succeeded in hiding themselves during the entire war.
Among the other tortured bodies that of Monsieur Franji is not found.
The body of Madame Franji is found.
She has nails driven into her gums.

The Milice arrested the neighborhood doctor.
At daybreak on a road leading out to the suburbs.
All four of his limbs broken.
His arms disjointed.
His legs disjointed.
Gashes on his face from a razor.
Fingers cut off.
They dumped him onto the road out of a moving car.

The Milice came and arrested a woman in the Resistance.
She was beaten.
She was raped.
They hung her in her house.

Philippe Henriot says and what if they did land?

They are landing.
—The hour for the settling of scores is about to strike someone says.

The bridges are blown up.
In the night they blew up all the bridges.
All except one.
The oldest.

Trucks filled with soldiers go past one behind the other.

You see hardly any more German soldiers in the streets.
You see lots of Milice in the streets.

Monsieur Lévy was dumped in front of his door.
Strangled.
His nails ripped out.

The Americans are advancing.

An old German soldier is sitting at the edge of the sidewalk. He has his legs apart. He has laid his helmet his knapsack and his rifle down next to him. He has white hair. Sagging shoulders, drooping arms. He is crying.
A woman says he's crying.
The husband replies that when the Americans weren't on their tails they didn't used to cry, they used to make others cry.

An old German soldier goes by on a bike. The jacket to his uniform is missing.

The Americans are advancing.

A fifteen-year-old German soldier comes walking along, the butt of his rifle dragging on the ground behind him. He does not know where he is going. He has his mouth open. He crosses the bridge. He sinks down from exhaustion. A man steps out of a house with a shotgun. He fires two shots. The body jumps two times under their impact.

They're tearing up the streets to make barricades and prevent the trucks of German soldiers from getting through.

In some sections they're setting buildings on fire.

The factory is closed.

The boss has disappeared.
The boss's partner has disappeared.
The foreman has disappeared.

We see the first FFI.
The women are hugging and kissing them.

The American tanks have a big white star.

The Americans they're saying.
The liberators they're saying.
The cowboys they're saying.
Uncle Sam they're saying.

To make themselves look good the bofs have signs

up in their windows saying they have products without tickets.

He is waiting for the trolley. It's a hot day. On the helmet he is wearing there is the emblem of the veterans' legion. He is in the shade close to the wall. The little square is almost deserted. The firing comes from the sidewalk opposite. The man sinks gradually downward on his jackknifing legs. There are two further shots. Two men run past. The helmet, tilted forward, is hiding the face of the dead man, on his knees, his back to the wall. You see no blood. His hands are on the ground, the palms upward. He has a watch on his wrist. The trolley arrives. People get out, pretending not to see. The sun has a reddish color.

—A few bofs there, they're going to be taken care of.
—With all that they put into their pockets while we were dying of hunger.
—Starvers of the people, every damned one of them.
—They never lacked for anything they themselves wanted.
—They're due to have their bellies slit.

The bofs are frightened.

The Americans are advancing.
—By God, if I'd had the time, I'd have given those Boche sons of bitches something to remember me by! More than once I was within an inch of joining the Resistance. You can ask my wife.

The wife says yes.

—My brother-in-law too, the bookkeeper, you know him? Oh man, was he ever Resistance! Let me tell you!

The wife says yes.

—The thing is, it would have meant having the time, and knowing some people.

The wife says yes.

Ever since it became known the Americans are on the way, everybody was in the Resistance.

A Jew, yes, everybody knew one.

A Jew they really liked.

A Jew to whom they lent a helping hand.

A good Jew.

A Jew they could have hidden had he asked.

For that matter they have an uncle who hid one.

Everybody hid Jews.

All the Jews I knew were tortured.

Deported.

Murdered.

A friend of mine found a khaki jacket with five stripes.

He's a colonel.

He has a rifle.

He says the baker's wife gave me nothing but grief during the whole damned war now I'm going after her skin.

They're all in the streets with their shotguns.

They've all been Gaullists since the beginning.

Since '40. Since day one.

De Gaulle spoke and they all heard his call.

A bof gave a lot without tickets and at the normal price to a Jew who was hiding in a room.

They weren't aware that they were engaging in black market activity.

They're here. Tanks. Trucks. Jeeps. All the bells are ringing. Girls up on the tanks. Girls inside the trucks. Girls in the jeeps. They're here. They shake hands. The crowd is enormous. The crowd roars Vive de Gaulle. The crowd roars Vive les Américains. The crowd roars Vive la Libération. There is jostling in the crowd. There is trampling in the crowd. Women are weeping. Men are weeping. The crowd's in each other's arms. It's the Americans. It's the GIs. We aren't good at pronouncing it. Everyone's crying. Laughing. Shouting. Clapping their hands. Singing. The crowd is in an unending roil. The crowd is ponderous. The crowd is enormous. Girls grab your head with both hands and run their tongue into your mouth. They do it to the one next to you. To the one next to him. The women are out of control. The women are out of control. The tanks are unable to proceed. The trucks are unable to proceed. The jeeps are unable to proceed. Engulfed by the crowd. Soldiers are shouting in American. The crowd replies OK. OK. The Americans laugh. On one tank an American is lifting a girl's skirt up to her waist and holding it there and she's laughing while shaking her head. The crowd is shouting the panties the panties. The girl crosses her hands over her sex. She is laughing. She sticks her tongue out at the crowd. The tanks inch ahead. In the jeeps the Americans have girls folded in their arms. They are kissing with mouths wide open. The crowd is yelling a kiss a kiss. Along come some French soldiers. The crowd yells Les Français les Français. The Americans are leading totally naked girls out of the rooms and onto the top-floor balcony of the grand hotel. They are fondling their breasts and slipping a hand between their thighs. They are bending them backward and kissing them. They are passing them back and forth to one another. The crowd roars. The crowd cheers. The crowd wants cigarettes. American ones. Inside the crowd a woman has thrown her brassiere up into the air. Inside the crowd a woman throws her panties up into the air. The crowd has massed tighter. The crowd is compressed. The crowd yells. The crowd is happy. The girls drag you through the crowd by the hand. The girls drag you by the hand into a secluded spot. The girls unbutton your fly. The girls take you in their mouth. The girls tell you I'm going to suck you all night long. The girls drown themselves in the crowd. The streets belong to the crowd. The avenues belong to the crowd. The squares belong to the crowd. The Americans are throwing chocolate bars. The crowd roars. The crowd reaches up to catch them. The Americans are throwing cans of food. K rations. The crowd is roaring. Hands are reaching up from the crowd to catch them. There is struggling in the crowd. The girls are trying to enter the Americans' hotels in order to get onto the balconies with them. By the entrance to the grand hotel are sentries with white helmets and the two letters MP. They say those ones are the tough ones. Maybe so. Who knows. The crowd is screaming. In the crowd people are dancing on the spot. The crowd is rubbing. There are hands at work frigging. The crowd is entwining. The crowd is making love to itself. On the quay at the water's edge soldiers are making love with women. There are some who are waiting for their turn. Underneath the bridges there is women's underwear. The crowd yells. The crowd coos. In a street set back a little three men are kicking another man to death. The cafés are packed. They've stopped letting any more in. The drinks are on the house. They're all singing dirty songs. It's the Liberation. It's the Americans. It's de Gaulle. It's France. There are three Milice hanging from trees. Their berets on their heads. There are some adolescents with shotguns. Other adolescents with shotguns. The crowd nothing but din. The crowd nothing but uproar. The crowd is shouting America America. The crowd is shouting Guynemer Guynemer. Some men wearing tricolored armbands kill a young man with their revolvers. In front of a shop window which flies to pieces. Night has come. The crowd sways. The crowd drifts, borne along by its flow. The people at the windows. The people who are yelling. The people who are singing. The crowd stirs with the stirrings of the night. The crowd is an enormous beast. Couples are lying on the sidewalks making love. Standing up against doors. On the grass that surrounds the memorial. Behind the gates. Women say hey you come here and give it to me. Women say I haven't any panties on. Women say just take me whatever way you want. The night is mild. The night is thick. The crowd moves off. Opposite the barracks where Americans now lodge the whorehouse is open. Red lantern lit. A whore in a short skirt on the threshold. Daylight is coming up.

My buddy in the Milice was shot.

The afternoon is dust and heat.
Heat of boredom.
I don't know what to do with myself this sultry summer afternoon.
There are few people in the street.
The people are off hiding.
The delivery van full of armed men arrives.
They are singing "Come along Ducky."
The delivery van squeals to a halt in front of the terrace outside the restaurant.
The armed men are shirtless.
They have a brassard on one arm.
They say they are FTP.
They are halfway drunk.
They jump out of the van.
They sing "Come along Ducky."
Bawl it out at the top of their lungs.
They want something to drink.
In the van there is a man who is bleeding.
They grab him by the shirt and pull him out.

He falls from the van.

He lets out a scream of pain.

He has one knee shattered by a bullet.

They say it's a son of a bitch collaborator.

They throw him onto a chair on the terrace.

The man's face is in shreds.

The man's face is black and blue.

The man is bleeding.

People come up for a look.

The people say it's a son of a bitch collaborator.

The leader has the movie actor Jules Berry's face tattooed on his chest.

Underneath the hair growing on his chest.

Pointing to his chest the leader tells the people I'm Jules Berry.

They are drinking beer.

From point-blank distance they take aim with a rifle at the bleeding man.

They are about to kill him.

I shut my eyes.

I put my hands over my ears.

They haven't killed him.

Jules Berry is slowly brushing the long barrel of a pistol over the man's forehead.

Jules Berry says to him tonight you son of a bitch you'll be dead.

Jules Berry says to him if I want you're dead this minute.

The people are all for that.

The dark woman arrives from the kitchen.

She is carrying an enameled basin filled with water.

She has a towel over her shoulder.

She is tall and severe.

She waves back the people clustered around the man who is bleeding.

Jules Berry tells her it's a son of a bitch collaborator.

Without saying anything she washes the man's wounds.

The water in the basin turns red.

The bleeding man kisses her hand.

Jules Berry pretends not to see.

The people have become still.

The heat is sticky.

The woman gives the bleeding man a glass of water.

Jules Berry says we're on a mission let's get going.

The dark woman carries the basin away to the kitchen.

The people are a little bit afraid.

The man who's bleeding is chucked into the van like a sack of flour.

He lets out a groan.

An old guy with white hair climbs up into the van.

He punches the man who's bleeding.

The man who's bleeding goes down onto the floor of the van.

The van starts up with a lot of backfiring.

They roll away.

They're singing "Come along Ducky."

They come along with the wife.

She is young.

She is crying.

They make her kneel down in the street.

The people gather around.

Piece of shit it sure as hell serves you right.

Piece of shit and you're not ashamed at having slept with a Boche.

She is kneeling down.

Punches.

Kicks.

They spit on her.

A man has hold of her shoulders.

A man has a pair of clippers in his hand.

The man clips off the kneeling woman's hair.

The people shout from joy.

The hair is falling all around the woman.

The woman is crying.

The people yell piece of shit.

The woman shuts her eyes.

Her hair is all clipped off.

The man strikes her on the head with the clippers.

Her head is bleeding.

Piece of shit get your ass out of here.

The woman staggers to her feet.

She receives kicks.

The woman is bleeding.

The woman is jeered and hooted at.

The woman puts a silk scarf over her head.

The women snatch her scarf away.

Women everywhere are having their hair clipped off.